All Shook Up

Natalie Stenzel

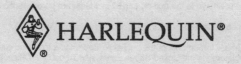

HARLEQUIN®

TORONTO • NEW YORK • LONDON
AMSTERDAM • PARIS • SYDNEY • HAMBURG
STOCKHOLM • ATHENS • TOKYO • MILAN • MADRID
PRAGUE • WARSAW • BUDAPEST • AUCKLAND

ISBN 0-373-44198-3

ALL SHOOK UP

ABOUT THE AUTHOR

Natalie Stenzel was a girl who just couldn't keep her nose out of (gasp!) a romance novel. Still, she denied her dreamy inclinations long enough to earn respectable degrees in English literature and magazine journalism from the University of Missouri-Columbia. She even flirted with business writing and freelancing for a while, considered going back to school for another respectable degree...only to return to her one true love: romance. Born and raised in St. Louis, Missouri, Natalie now resides in lovely Virginia with her husband and two children, happy to live a dream (or several) come true.

Books by Natalie Stenzel

HARLEQUIN FLIPSIDE
 4—FORGET PRINCE CHARMING
12—POP-UP DATING

To the loopy riders.
You know who you are.
My sanity requires you.
Thank you.

1

"Is it true?"

Fighting the pull of a green-eyed stare from across the restaurant, Marley Brentwood kept her gaze squarely on the man sitting across from her. "Dad? You didn't, did you?"

Charles Brentwood set his fork down and sighed. "Now, honey. That's an exaggeration of the facts. I would never—"

"Oh my God. You did." She stared at her father in horror. She'd expected him to laugh at the very idea. It was so crazy, so throwback. Even for him. Her cheeks hot, she dropped her napkin on the table and eyed the nearest exit.

"Marley." Her father turned that intimidating look on her, the one that normally gained him whatever he wanted. "Just settle down so we can discuss this. You're being irrational."

Irrational. The biggest crime in her father's eyes. So be it.

She shoved her chair back and grabbed her purse. "Unbelievable. You actually *bought* my fiancé for me." Her voice rose in pitch and volume. "And *I'm* the irrational one?"

"I did not 'buy' you a fiancé, Marley."

"No, you just offered Larry one hell of a promotion and a whopping raise. *Effective on our wedding date and conditional upon two years of wedded bliss.*"

"Marley—"

She overrode him. "Looks like, quacks like, *stinks* like a *purchased fiancé* to me."

Her father just gaped, his shock still eclipsing the anger that was sure to follow.

And no wonder. She *never* used that tone of voice with him. For as long as she could remember, she'd obeyed his every dictate, striven for perfection. She had always aimed for his approval, both on the job and off.

And look where it had gotten her. Nowhere.

She stood up and looped her purse over her shoulder. "You can tell my pricey fiancé that we're through, and while you're at it—" She paused, briefly considered, then went with it. Offering him a fiercely composed smile, she spoke crisply. "You can tell Human Resources that I resign from my position as marketing director of your company. Effective immediately."

Ignoring his outraged protests, she stalked toward the exit, vaguely aware—and not giving a damn—that a tall, green-eyed jerk a few tables over also had stood up, no doubt to follow her again. He'd be regretting *that* soon enough.

On that vicious thought, she shoved the door open and veered sharply right on busy Carey Street in the heart of downtown Richmond, Virginia. The heart-thumping staccato of her own high heels against bricked sidewalk was somehow satisfying in her rage. God knows she deserved *some* satisfaction.

It was so damned hard to believe. Even of someone as backward-thinking as her father. He'd actually *paid* Larry to propose to her. And he thought that *she* was the irrational one? That she shouldn't be upset because he'd used his money to arrange her life for her? "Of all the damned *arrogance.*"

Another pedestrian slowed to stare and she glared a dismissal. "Not *you*." The man raised his hands, implying complete harmlessness, and stopped to let her pass.

She didn't alter her pace, for once not caring what kind of scene she might be making. Hell, it wasn't as if she had any dignity left to preserve anyway.

What had her father been *thinking?* Did he really believe no guy would want her without a cash incentive to sweeten the deal?

A frustrated exhale hissed through her teeth, inviting another startled stare, which she ignored.

Of course that's what her father thought. She wasn't exactly attracting hordes of panting men. Hell, she'd rarely even *dated* before Larry. And there was her father making stupid noises about how she'd *soon see the end of her twenties*. Gee, wasn't it time to get married and pop out babies before menopause kicked her in the ass?

Like *that* should be her only calling in life. As if she should marry the kind of guy who required a hefty *bribe* to walk down the aisle with her. Ha. If her father was so desperate for litters of young, he should buy a *dog* and put it up for stud.

Although, apparently, he'd tried to do exactly that. Marley ground her teeth, feeling a little feral herself. *Here, Larry. Good dog. Have a biscuit. Go marry my daughter now.*

Oh, and speaking of beastly studs, what about Josh? How the hell would she ever face *that* man again? He knew the truth: her father paid Larry to propose to her. Hell, Josh was the one who'd clued her in on the situation in the first place, though she'd refused to believe him initially. Well, he'd been right. Two points for Josh the Omniscient. God, how humiliating.

Especially given a socially excruciating incident

that happened months ago. It still killed her to recall her mild—pathetic, really—attempt to flirt with him at a coffee shop near the headquarter offices of Brentwood Electronics. At that point, she hadn't known who he was, but, *ugh*. The memory just sent her temper raging higher. Heaven *forbid* she take just one *tiny* little step onto the wild side, talking up a stunningly gorgeous stranger just for entertainment and minor thrills.

Only to have her targeted stud respond with a dismissive little smile. He'd barely even noticed her.

Naturally, tall, sexy and oblivious had turned out to be none other than Joshua T. Walker, her father's newest vice *peon*. Her ego reeling, she'd tried to ignore him on anything but a professional level ever since. Even harder on her ego was the inevitable brain scramble she experienced whenever they occupied the same office or meeting room. To compensate for any awkwardness, she was probably curt to the point of rudeness whenever she had to speak to him.

So why had he concluded that it was *his* duty to enlighten her with the ugly truth? She'd have taken the news about Larry and her father better from anyone but Josh. *Anyone* else.

And now, if that weren't enough, after breaking the news to her, apparently he'd felt the need to tail her to the restaurant and play spectator while she confronted her father. Why? Just to complete her humiliation? Perhaps he was short on cheap entertainment for the afternoon? Well, she'd certainly provided that. How lovely for him.

Sure, he'd sat at another table, but he must have overheard every word she'd said. Probably everyone else in the restaurant had, too—

"Marley, wait!"

Hearing the familiar masculine voice and footsteps hurrying behind her, she picked up her own pace. Great. Just what was needed to top off the day from hell. *Josh*. Well, not if she could help it. She turned to cross—

Josh caught her arm before she stepped blindly into traffic, too angry to see the cab flying by, horn blaring.

She inhaled sharply, recovered, then tugged free and began hurrying across the street, angry but aware now.

"Slow down, Marley." Josh kept his voice quiet but firm. He'd had to hustle to catch her. Hell, if he'd arrived a moment later, she might be roadkill even now. And it would be at least partly his fault.

"Why? So you can say 'I told you so' about a matter that was never *your* business in the first place?" She glanced briefly at him before turning and striding toward a nearby parking lot. "You're entitled. Go right ahead." She spoke low, her expression composed, but for the fury blazing in those golden eyes of hers. "Just make it fast and then leave me alone."

Josh groaned inwardly. Sometimes it really sucked to be the messenger. But she was pissed and she had a right to be. He spoke low. "How about an 'I'm sorry'?"

She halted and met his eyes. "Don't you dare." Her voice was a hoarse whisper. So different from the cool, silky tones he was used to hearing from her. The woman was definitely pissed, that gorgeous auburn hair seeming to spark with her rage, cheeks flushed, eyes snapping with fury. She was so alive. Animated.

Marley. It was hard not to stare. There she was.

And she was glaring at him, as though she'd like nothing better than to take a swing at someone. *Him.* Damn.

"I don't need or want your pity." She raised her eyebrows, the look in her eyes as nervy as any he'd ever seen on a woman. "What I want is my car and a ride the hell out of here."

"Let me drive you, then. In this mood, you'll only kill yourself…or someone else."

"No." She turned on a heel and marched into the parking lot. When he continued to follow her to her car, she pulled out her keys and spoke without looking at him. "Isn't your lunch break about over yet? Oh, but wait. You veep types enjoy flexible hours, don't you. Yet another *executive perk*."

"Cut it out, Marley." He kept his voice even. "I didn't take the deal. Larry did."

She whipped a horrified gaze up to meet his. "My father tried to buy *you*, too?"

Josh could have kicked himself. Marley was smart as hell and it would behoove his asinine brain to remember that before speaking. "That's beside the point."

"Unbelievable." With a jerky laugh, she shook her head and slid behind the wheel. "Well, I guess we can't accuse him of favoritism. You both got a shot at the 'promotion.'"

"It wasn't like that, Marley." He gripped the car door. "Come on, slide over and let me drive."

"Hands off or I'll slam the door on them."

Hearing sure intent in her evenly spaced words, Josh yanked his hands back just as the door slammed shut. Damn. She hadn't even hesitated, or— The car roared to life and he stepped back smartly as she jerked it into Reverse and backed out of the parking space. The little sedan screeched into traffic, amid honks of protest, and disappeared around a corner.

"Well, that went well." Josh shook his head in self-disgust. Concerned, he climbed into his own car and discreetly followed Marley to her apartment in the West End.

Once she'd safely parked and entered her building, he turned his sights back to the road. As much as he hated leaving her alone, he knew she'd never listen to him now. He'd stop by after work, once she had a chance to cool down.

After a last reluctant glance at her apartment building, he eased back into traffic, still cursing through a list of regrets. He should have found some way to break things off between Marley and Larry Donatelli besides telling her the humiliating truth.

Though he hated to admit it, Josh figured there was no way Marley wanted to hear about her fiancé from Josh, of all people. For reasons he still pondered, Marley regarded him with suspicion, if not outright hostility. He'd venture to add dislike, except for some contrary reason, he didn't think so.

He signaled for a turn, accelerated and merged onto the parkway. As traffic eased, he let his thoughts wander further. Marley. She'd been so different today. Hell, ever since his first day at Brentwood Electronics, the woman had intrigued him. He hadn't known why or pursued it at first. He wasn't a kid, after all, and he knew the perils of crushing on the boss's daughter. But gradually, inklings had grown into assurance then blossomed into absolute fascination with the woman.

Sure, Marley was beautiful, but that was just the beginning of it.

No, the woman was *smart*—probably smarter than she ever let on to herself or others. It showed in the way she did business, and in the slick way she got around her father when necessary. Even in the way she handled him, Josh, when she thought he didn't notice.

She worked for her father's company, and Charles Brentwood was as old-fashioned as a crusty old patriarch could get—as was his company. Not a simple obstacle, but she handled it with such skill, that a less observant man could almost be forgiven for thinking the obstacle didn't exist.

Josh, however, had always prided himself on his observation skills. He wanted nothing more than a chance to put them to up-close and personal use. With Marley.

Still, time and again, he'd tried to initiate a casual conversation with her at work, but she always just breezed by him with a polite, dismissive word. She always had someplace else she needed to be.

And yet, he'd seen her joking with her assistant, warm and witty with other co-workers, male and female. Why did he, Josh, always get the cold shoulder?

Especially when he could have sworn that once upon a time she'd actually flirted with him a little. That was before they'd been introduced, though, and at the time, he'd been sweating a little over his new job and his intentions. He'd wished ever since then that he'd at least flirted back. Paved the way just a bit. But he hadn't. And she'd had not one flirtatious word for him ever since then, no matter what he'd tried.

So, he'd watched in frustration as she got herself engaged to Larry, then waited with even more frustration as her wedding day crept closer and closer. During darker moments, he even dared to regret turning down Charles's outrageous proposition that *Josh* be the one to date and marry Marley.

Screw the money and the promotion—Josh had other plans, after all—but he did want a shot with Marley. Given the chance, Charles might have made an effective, if clumsy, matchmaker. After all, he'd managed to get Larry and Marley together, a match even Josh could see was a bad fit.

But, no, Josh had stuck to his high-principled, and possibly high-*ego'd*, guns. He wanted Marley, but he'd be damned if he made it part of some ass-backward business merger.

Then, this morning, Marley had chosen a particularly bad moment to waltz into his office with a distant smile and legs longer than the raunchiest of his dreams, to drop off a copy of the marketing report. He'd only just learned about the weekend getaway she and Donatelli had planned, and sweet reason had fled to points unknown. He just couldn't stomach the thought of Marley in bed with scum like Larry.

Or any other man for that matter.

So, he'd lost his cool and detained Marley long enough to tell her a few things about her *fiancé.* She'd pivoted on one businesslike heel, and, as he'd discovered just now, she'd demanded the truth from her father—not Donatelli.

And that was the single point of light in this whole bleak mess. Josh just had to believe that a woman in love would have confronted her *fiancé* first, not her father.

AFTER CHANGING out of her work clothes, Marley faced the unusual prospect of an entire weekday afternoon at home. Away from work. And with so damn much frenetic energy on her hands she'd like to crawl right out of her skin. So she took it out on her apartment, scrubbing floors and polishing windows and mirrors until they shone.

Once she'd exhausted the worst of it, she took a scalding hot shower. Then she forced herself to sit down and be rational about her position. She was, after all, out of work now. It was time for closure and follow-up.

Still restless but focused now, she put on a pot of coffee and sat down to compose a formal letter of resignation. After carefully checking it for errors, she slid it into an envelope and dropped it in the mailbox—next to a smaller envelope with a one-and-a-half-carat bulge in its side.

She supposed it was less than rational to drop a diamond ring in the mail as if it were worth no more than the postage stamped on the envelope.

Maybe it was even a little *ir*rational.

Fine.

Good, in fact.

She slammed the mailbox shut and returned to her apartment to browse the classifieds. Briefly, she allowed herself to feel a little wistful about quitting her job. She'd had to do it, but the timing…

She grimaced. She'd just gotten into the heart of the Blaylock project, a major undertaking she'd tackled with enthusiasm but hadn't fully discussed with her father as yet. It still required special handling. And so did her father.

Mentally, she shrugged and forced herself to let it go. It was no longer her responsibility. Larry could deal with the project—and her father. She'd worry about relaying the contents of her briefcase later, when she felt up to dealing with any of the male rats in her life. And as for her own attachment to the Blaylock deal, the challenge of it… Well, there would be other challenges.

She would see to it.

Frowning over a fresh cup of coffee, Marley circled an ad for a marketing coordinator. Promising, she decided. It merited a phone call, at least. Just as she popped the lid back on her highlighter, the telephone rang.

"Hello?" She spoke absently, still scanning columns of fine print. *Director of marketing…hmm.* She popped the lid off again and slashed bright yellow across it, too.

"Marley. What are you doing at home?" Larry sounded baffled and mildly annoyed. "We had a one o'clock meeting today and you never showed."

Marley glanced up from the ad, feeling her stomach muscles knot up all over again. What *was* that feeling anyway? Anger, maybe? Well. How about that? Cool, composed little Marley had rediscovered her temper—and that it had staying power.

"Larry. How nice of you to call." Her voice saccharine, she carefully recapped the pen and set it down.

"Well, damn it, you didn't show up. I thought we had an understanding. Now that your Dad thinks the sun rises and sets in Walker's office, you're my biggest ally in the company. Hell, Brentwood won't even listen to me without your backing. And you didn't show. You let me down."

Pompous asshole was actually chiding *her* for disloyalty? *Un*believable. "Gosh, Larry, funny you should mention alliances and business in the same breath."

After a silent moment, he exhaled roughly. "Okay, I get it. You're upset about the promotion your father offered me."

"Oh, you heard. I'm *so* relieved."

"You're overreacting, Marley. This wasn't some underhanded scheme intended to hurt you in any way."

"Then what was it?"

"It was…a simple business agreement based on my—my new position of *trust* in your father's company."

Marley gave an un-Marley-like snort.

"Come on. Be reasonable, Marley." Larry's voice rose in mild annoyance. "Deals like this happen all the time in the business world. And you have to know how much that promotion would mean to me. Think about it. In this higher position, I might even have a chance at unseating Walker as your dad's right-hand man. I'd have new leverage."

"Oh, I'm sorry. Maybe I should have considered your career path before I broke our engagement.

Where *are* my priorities?" She glared at the phone before returning it to her ear.

"I—" He stopped.

"Yes?" It was a challenge.

He just sighed. "You're right. I'm sorry. I'm being completely insensitive."

Finally. Someone exhibiting signs of sanity in her world. "Yes, you are."

"It must have been a shock for you. Hearing everything like that. Especially if you went to the boss for explanations." He laughed, a little uncomfortably. "Your father and mine should get together and have an arrogance party, hey?"

She didn't reply.

He hesitated, then spoke softly, coaxingly. "Look, Marley. I'm sorry if this hurt you. Or embarrassed you. But I think you're viewing this situation in the worst possible light. It's not all black-and-white. Just because there are some substantial gains to be made doesn't mean it wouldn't be a good marriage, too. I really do like and respect you. I always have. And, frankly, I still think we'd do well together."

"You've got to be kidding. You really think I'd marry you still, knowing where it all started? With cash and a promotion? *Get real.* I may have been blind and gullible up to this point, but that load of bricks hit me pretty *damn* hard today."

"Come on, just think about it, Marl. *Please.* We could have a great life together. And one day your father would retire and we'd be in control of his company. Together. We'd be the ultimate power couple, and—"

Her stomach heaved at the thought. "Forget it, Larry. We're through. Period."

"Marley! You can't do this. You know what this could mean for me." Bitterness crept into his voice. "Hell, I could even show *my* father, arrogant bastard, that once and for all—"

So that was it. He was one-upping Daddy Donatelli, and he wanted to use her and her father's company to do it. Not in this lifetime. "So sorry about the lost promotion, Larry. Better luck next time." She tried for a blasé tone, was almost sure she pulled it off. "*Such* a shame that you'll have to rethink your strategy, though. Now that I'm off the market, my father's *all* out of salable daughters." The last ended on a brittle singsong.

"I—" Larry halted mid tirade. "Um. Marley? Have you been drinking?" He sounded uncertain all of a sudden, even alarmed. "This isn't like you. You're usually so levelheaded, so—"

"Rational?"

"Yeah. Rational. *Completely.* I just—" She heard him exhale in heavy frustration. "I don't know how to talk to you in this mood. Maybe you ought to just, um, sleep it off or something."

"Sure. Why not? Bye, Larry. Your ring's in the mail." She hung up to his shocked protests. "Jerk."

Oh, but it felt good to kiss him off like that. He had it coming. Now, maybe she could work in peace and quiet. In fact, she'd ensure just that. She reached for the phone's base.

Before she could turn the ringer off, the phone rang again, almost immediately. Groaning over possibilities—her father? Larry hitting redial?—she just let the machine get it. After the tinny version of her own voice invited a short message, she heard the familiar sound of her cousin's voice on the line.

Relieved, she picked up. "Hi, Samantha."

"Marley! Are you sick? I called your office and they said you left work early today. You never leave work early."

The concern in Sammi's voice soothed her. "No, I'm not sick. I resigned."

"You resigned? From your *job?*"

"Yeah. At lunch today."

"*Nooo.*"

At the scandalized tone in her cousin's voice, Marley almost smiled. "Yep. I really did. I quit my job, my engagement, and very probably, the city itself. I guess we'll see what the job search turns up." As shocking as the words sounded on her own lips, Marley couldn't deny the heady feeling that something inside her had finally broken free.

It actually felt good. In a naughty kind of way. How *irresponsible* of her to quit her job before finding another one.

"Do *not* move." Sammi sounded urgent. "I'm coming over." The line clicked.

Not ten minutes later, the doorbell rang, and Marley glanced up in surprise. "Wow. That was fast." She smiled. Good. She needed nothing more right now than Sammi's outrageousness and die-hard loyalty. She should have called her immediately.

Still smiling, she swung the door open. And nearly slammed it closed again. "*You.* Why?"

It was Josh, his broad shoulders filling the doorway and calm determination written all over his too handsome face. "I was worried about you."

When she opened her mouth to either welcome or curse, the phone started ringing again. She glanced back at it, then raised an inquiring eyebrow at her unwelcome guest. "And I suppose that's my father on the phone now?"

"I wouldn't be surprised." Not waiting for an invitation, he brushed past her and reached for the phone himself.

"Just what do you think you're doing?"

"Sparing you." Then he held up a casually silencing finger, thereby boosting her blood pressure all over again. *Anger.* Truly an amazing concept. She could really do something with that.

"Charles? Yeah, I'm here... No, I won't... I wouldn't recommend it... No, I'll let you handle that. File's on my desk. Bye." He dropped the phone into its cradle, then turned back to face her.

Marley gestured with arms stretched wide, her baffled outrage nearly robbing her of words. "In case it escaped your notice, we're in my apartment, *not* your office. When the phone rings, *I* answer it, not you."

He gave her a rueful look and sighed. "I know. And I pissed you off again. I only answered it because I knew it would be your father on the line and I was afraid another encounter between you two would be fatal. For somebody."

Her raised eyebrow implied that the fatality might have been—could still be—*Josh*. "What did he want?"

"Among other things, he wanted you to come back to work tomorrow. I didn't think that was in the cards and told him as much. He didn't argue."

She gave him a cynical look. "He always argues."

"Yeah, usually." His mouth curved slightly. "But this time, I think he's relieved that I'm here instead of him. I don't think he knows how to deal with you right now."

"Of course he doesn't. I understand I'm *overreacting*. Being *unreasonable*. Even alarmingly *impulsive*." She almost sneered the words, the memory igniting her temper all over again. "So I suppose *you* think I'm being irrational, too? That I should continue to work for my father, now that he's undermined me both personally and professionally?"

Josh slid his hands into the pockets of his suit pants and regarded her thoughtfully. "No. Given the circumstances, I think you've been surprisingly rational about all this."

Her fury seemed to hit a brick wall. She stared at

him. "Surprisingly rational. Huh. You know at this point in time, I don't know whether to be offended by that statement or not."

He chuckled, his green eyes twinkling appreciatively. "Actually, it's my opinion that everyone's entitled to the occasional impulse, irrational or otherwise." His voice deepened. "So what's yours going to be?"

"My what?"

His lashes lowered, concealing all but a gleam of humor. "Your irrational impulse. Hell, if anyone's entitled to one right now, it's you. Look where rational thought got you."

A wry grin tugged briefly at her lips. "Unengaged and unemployed. Good point." After a moment, she narrowed her eyes. "That's an annoying habit of yours, by the way." At his silent question, she grudgingly clarified. "Being right."

He nodded. "For what it's worth, I am sorry you had to get hurt by all this. But I still think you're better off without Donatelli. And frankly, I think your father's needed a good shock where you're concerned. You gave it to him. He was looking a little rough this afternoon."

Some of her ire returning at mention of her father, Marley raised her chin. "He should. Old-fashioned is one thing. This—what he did—that crosses the line." She shook her head, waving a hand as though she could erase the outrageous act. "I still cannot believe— And *why* am I telling you all this?" She tossed up her hands and stared past him at the wall.

Josh rubbed the back of his neck, then gestured vaguely. "Look. I think your father's intentions were good. He just wants to see you settled. Comfortably."

"And he's willing to pay cold, hard cash to see it happen." She spoke evenly and without hesitation.

Josh winced. "Hey, don't blame me. If I approved

of what he was doing, I never would have told you about it."

Sighing, she dropped onto the couch and tucked her feet under her. "Yeah. I suppose I do owe you for that." And admitting as much was bitter as hell.

Sweeping back the hem of his suit coat, Josh seated himself on the arm of the couch, mere inches away from and above her. He tipped his head to the side to study her. "Now that's an interesting way of looking at matters. Generous, too, considering I was the hated bearer of bad news. So you owe me, huh?" He smiled thoughtfully. "When can I expect to collect?"

She gave him a wary look. "What do you mean?"

"How about going to dinner with me? Tonight."

She shook her head in a vain attempt to clear her mind of what she couldn't possibly have just heard. *"What?"*

"Damn, but you're hard on a man's ego. I asked you out to dinner. A date." He grinned, just a little sheepishly. "Hell, you could always accept and just chalk it up as your allotted irrational impulse."

"You're kidding. A *date?*" She narrowed her eyes. "Who's paying? My father?"

He smiled, but it lacked humor. "Now you're pissing me off. I don't take payoffs. Especially not from the father of a woman I—" He broke off and grimaced.

"A woman you…*what?*" She gave him a look, one that dared he finish his statement.

He studied her for a moment, his lips twisting ironically. "A woman I'm attracted to."

2

"YOU'RE WHAT?"

"I'm attracted to you, Marley." Josh shrugged, his words simple, his eyes searching.

She pulled away sharply, then stood up to stare down at him. "You're asking me out." She shook her head slowly, baffled and rejecting. "*Now?* Couldn't you even wait until the engagement was cold?" She narrowed her eyes. "Wait. Did you tell me about Larry and my dad…just so you could *date* me? That's *sick.*"

"No. I would have told you regardless." He shrugged. "But asking you out is something I should have done long before now. I've wanted to for months." He continued to watch her, his body still but tense.

She shook her head, rejecting all of it. "You're crazy. The whole world's gone crazy."

"Think so?" He tilted his head slightly, his eyes narrowed and focused completely on her.

She stared. Reluctantly. That little smile, the gleam of curiosity, interest, humor in his eyes…*so* appealing.

Oh, she was *such* an idiot. As irrational and illogical as her father ever claimed she was. She groaned silently. "I think you should leave. This is really *not* a good time."

"There she is. Rational, always professional Marley. Despite all the insults, the sarcasm, the temper, I knew you were still hanging on to her." His voice, oddly enough, was teasing again. "I tell you I'm attracted to you and you tell me 'this is not a good time.' " His smile widened. "Priceless."

"Don't you mean 'frigid'?" Her words dripped with ice.

"Oh, Lord, no. Not frigid. *Reserved,* maybe. But there's a helluva spark there."

Spark? Inside *Marley Brentwood?* She clenched her teeth to keep her jaw from dropping open—again.

He raised an eyebrow. "I suppose some bonehead called you frigid because you wouldn't fall into bed with him?"

She didn't respond, although a resounding *yes* would have been eerily appropriate. The guy was Larry, and after she'd sidled out of lovemaking a few weeks ago, he'd lost his temper and called her an "ice queen." Later, he'd apologized, chalked the incident up to stress and suggested the need for a romantic getaway. Still, his words had haunted her, mostly because she was afraid he was right.

Not that she intended to share any of that experience with Josh. The man had witnessed quite enough of her humiliation in the past few days.

Josh stood up, and the overhead lights gleamed off his dark, closely trimmed hair. When he began his approach, she stiffened but refused to retreat any farther.

Damn it, this was *her* apartment.

"Marley, Marley. Don't you know better than to believe a man who claims a woman is frigid?"

She didn't respond, but found it difficult to breathe. When had she thought this man was bloodless? Was she *blind?* Good grief, but the man was hot, hot, hot—*way* out of her league. And now he was casually closing in on her, to stop just a breathless foot away. Cautiously, knowing she had no choice, she raised her gaze to meet his.

He was looking down at her with a little smile that managed to be both sexy and teasingly confiding. "Let me share a little secret from the brotherhood of men with you."

She forced a glare, scrambling for an appropriate retort.

"Hush, Marley. This is good stuff. Hell, I could even get kicked out of the club for blowing our collective cover."

She narrowed her eyes and raised a skeptical eyebrow. "A secret. Among men. I can hardly wait."

He grinned. "Well, it is actually a simple one. Ready?"

She sighed with forced patience.

He nodded, his grin fading to speculation. "Okay, here it is—*there's no such thing as an inherently frigid woman.*" He paused to let her absorb his words. "A man only calls a woman frigid when he's feeling the sting of his *own* failure."

Her eyebrows shot up in surprise. "Failure?"

"Yes, failure. It's the man's responsibility...and pleasure—" his gaze drifted to her mouth "—to arouse the woman."

"I see." Stunned and completely disarmed, she could manage only a faint response. "So I guess you've never accused a woman...of being frigid?"

He smiled slowly, wickedly, his eyes conveying a wealth of tantalizing experience. "I've never had cause to."

She stared a moment, speechless, then groaned, low and frustrated. "Heaven help me, but I'm going to positively *kill* the next arrogant man I meet today."

"Huh." His eyes sparkled with laughter. "Too much information for you?"

"I think you'd better leave." She glared at him. "Before my homicidal tendencies get the best of me."

"Okay, okay." He paused. "Just one question first and then I'll go. Peacefully. I swear."

"Make it good."

His smile faded. "You quit your job. What are you going to do now?"

"Find another job."

He nodded. "I have some connections. Why don't I—"

She stiffened. "No, thank you. I have connections of my own. I don't need or want help from you or anyone else in my father's company. Now, *out*."

"Okay, okay. I'll call you in the morning."

"That's not necessary." She stood aside and opened the door. The man was her father's vice president. Anything beyond that fact was moot. Her father owned him.

"I said I'll call you." His voice was as implacable as his expression.

"Fine. Call me." She wouldn't answer the phone.

He eyed her narrowly but, to her relief, just turned toward the door. When she would have closed it behind him, he stopped her with a simple palm laid flat against the wood.

"What?"

"Just this. Whatever you do, don't sell yourself short. You've worked in your father's shadow for a long time now, and I get the feeling you're capable of a lot more than that."

Disarmed by the unexpected vote of confidence, Marley stared out into the hallway long minutes after Josh had left. Finally, annoyed at her preoccupation with the man and his cheap philosophy, she slammed the door closed.

When the doorbell rang again ten minutes later, she cast a suspicious glance through the peephole before answering it. She could have wept at the welcome sight of Sammi standing there in the flesh.

"I brought reinforcements." Sammi held up a bag of potato chips. "Cheap carbs will cure *anything*."

Thirty minutes later, the cousins were both shoeless and lounging on Marley's cherry-wood-trimmed couch, the bag of chips lying open between them and already half-gone. Thanks to Sammi's company and unconditional support during the retelling of events, Marley felt a whole hell of a lot better. The chips hadn't hurt, either.

"So then you just *quit?*" Samantha gaped at her cousin, the light of unholy amusement glittering in her eyes. "*Adios?* Just like that?"

"You don't have to sound so excited about the whole thing, Sammi." Marley reached for another chip. "It *was* my life that went up in smoke today. All my plans. My job, my wedding. Everything. And, since I'm no longer going to the mountains with Larry, so much for my ski vacation. *Damn it.* I think even my plane tickets were nonrefundable." She frowned. "I wonder if the airline would exchange them."

She looked up, saw her cousin was still grinning, and lowered her eyebrows repressively. "Sammi!"

"I can't help it, Marley. I'm just thrilled for you. This is exactly what you needed. A fresh start. Free from your father's puppet strings, free from that plastic mimbo of a ladder climber you called a fiancé—"

Marley's eyes widened. "*What* did you call him?" The phrase sounded just like one Josh had used this morning, though he might have added a few off-color adjectives.

Samantha rolled her eyes. "Ladder climber? Or plastic mimbo?" She gestured in remembered disgust. "Come on, Marley. Even I could tell the guy had an agenda."

Marley shrugged. "We all have an agenda of some kind. And agenda or no, I think you still underestimate him. He had his good points. And God knows we could relate when it came to overbearing fathers. His was worse than mine. It's a wonder Larry turned out as well as he did."

"Maybe." Sammi sounded doubtful. "But he crossed the line when his agenda involved using you."

"No argument there." Marley scowled, remembering. "I can't believe I didn't see what was going on. That he didn't really want me just for *me.* You saw it. Josh saw it. Why didn't I? Am I some kind of blind idiot?"

"What, for getting engaged to him?" At Marley's nod, she shrugged. "Nah. I prefer to think you were just naive."

"Naive? Give me a break, Sammi."

"I'm serious. You *are* naive. At least when it comes to the man-woman thing."

Marley sighed, feeling depressed. "Considering how Larry fooled me, I guess I can't argue with that. I think the word you were looking for, though, is *gullible.*"

"Oh, lighten up, will you?" Samantha smiled at her a little, eyes twinkling. "So, he was trash. Big deal. You took out the garbage. End of story. You obviously didn't love him or we'd be wading through your tears right now." She paused, eyebrows raised.

Marley nodded, conceding the point. "Dad liked him."

Sammi rolled her eyes. "Like that's an endorsement."

Marley grinned. "Okay, we can go back to *idiot,* then, too."

"*Naive.* As in, lack of experience. Think about it. What do you know about marriage, anyway? Your mom's been gone since you were a little kid, and your father's definitely on the reserved side of fuzzy. He's not the kind of daddy to tell a little girl stories about love and commitment, that kind of thing."

"No. He's not." Marley spoke thoughtfully.

Samantha warmed to her subject. "The way I see it, you were bound to screw up the first time around. Look at it this way. At least you found out before the wedding."

Marley rolled her eyes. "No kidding." She paused before going back to something that had bugged her. "What did you mean by 'puppet strings'?"

Samantha winced. "Did I actually say that? I mean, I didn't intend to actually *say* it like that. It sounds worse than—"

"Just spit it out. You've never pulled punches before."

"Much you know. But okay." She paused before proceeding with more than customary delicacy. "Marl. Has it ever occurred to you that your father's a little…*domineering?*"

Marley snorted. "You think this is news to me? Of course he's domineering."

"And that maybe you let him walk all over you sometimes?"

That hurt. A bit. She sighed. "Okay, there might be some truth in that."

"Or maybe a whole lot of truth in it?"

Marley tugged on a lock of hair dangling by her ear. "Okay. Maybe a lot. He's my father. He's all I've had for most of my life, and maybe he's used to telling me what to do and I'm used to doing what he tells me. Mostly. Unless I can get around him without causing an uproar."

"So, just to be clear…you've never actually defied the man—and we're talking true rebellion, here—

until now." Samantha gave her a hard stare, those big blue eyes steady and meaningful.

"Until now. You're right." Marley nodded, then spoke with more conviction. "I've always done what was expected of me. Until now." She looked up, her eyes widening, even as she felt an outrageous grin spread across her face. "And it feels...*so* good."

Samantha laughed. "Welcome to adolescence, darling."

"Adolescence, my ass. I'm almost thirty."

"Twenty-eight."

"Same difference."

Samantha smiled. "Not quite, but we'll let that stand. So what are you going to do now? Break curfew? Take up smoking?"

"You're impossible." Marley laughed at her. Still, something inside bubbled and tingled. Freedom. It felt like freedom. As it threatened to spill over into something scary, she slammed a lid on it. Still, her heart pounded. "I'm not sure what I'm going to do yet. I'll have to think about it."

"Good. You do that. And have some fun, too, why don't you. It's time."

Marley pondered. Intensely. "Yes. Yes, it is."

"Good. Name the time and place, and I'm *there*. We'll cause all kinds of trouble." She flashed Marley a wicked grin, then glanced at the clock. "But. As much as I'd like to sit here and stir up trouble with you now, I really have to go. I'm leaving for the weekend with Roger tomorrow, and I really need to pack a few things before falling in bed tonight." She flashed a brilliant smile at Marley.

Marley stood, too, feeling something tighten inside of her. It might have been jealousy, as unworthy as that was. "A date for the weekend? Where are you going?"

"I'm not sure yet." Samantha's eyes twinkled naughtily.

"You're going away for the weekend with a man you met less than a month ago. And you're not sure where he's taking you."

"Not a clue. I don't think he knows, either."

"So you're just going to hop in the car—"

"Motorcycle." Samantha grinned.

Marley shook her head slowly, laughing. "You are so bad, Samantha." And envy was eating away at her insides.

"It's not a crime to do something wild, just for the hell of it." Samantha raised an eyebrow at her before turning to leave. "You should try it sometime."

SAMANTHA'S SUGGESTION echoed over and over in Marley's head, while she typed up job-application letters, and throughout a mostly restless night. And the more she considered the idea, the more it made sense. Life was meant to be lived. It was an adventure to be experienced firsthand—not vicariously, as she'd done all these years through Sammi's exploits.

As the sun rose, so did Marley's mood and her hopes. And her daring. Maybe, just maybe, it was time good-girl Marley had a bad-girl adventure of her own.

The question was, how did a good girl find her way into an adventure? Suddenly, she remembered the plane ticket to Denver that she wouldn't be using now that she'd broken up with Larry. Would a stay in Colorado satisfy this lust for adventure?

She thought about the mountains and the cold. Larry. Her wedding plans. No, Denver was out. Besides, everyone knew she'd planned the trip.

So she'd exchange her plane ticket and travel somewhere else entirely. On that thought, she climbed out of bed, took a quick shower and hauled her breakfast into the extra bedroom she used as an occasional office. Then she turned on the computer.

Almost giddy now and trying to tamp it down, Marley picked up the phone and hit speed dial. "Sammi? Will you water my plants on Monday if I'm not back?"

"Um, sure." Samantha sounded puzzled. "God, it's barely eight o'clock. Do you have a job interview already? Fast work."

"No interview. I'm going on an adventure." Marley watched the monitor as her computer warmed up.

Silence. "You're going to do what?"

"I've decided you're right, Sammi. All my life, I've planned, I've taken precautions, I've followed rules, I've been *rational*. And look where it's gotten me? So, I'm going to be a little…*ir*rational now."

"Okay, you're starting to scare me."

Quickly typing in her password, Marley laughed. "Why? You're the one who gave me the idea."

"So where are you going, then?"

"I don't know yet."

"Who's going with you?"

"No one."

"See? *That's* how you're scaring me."

"Come on, Samantha. I'm an adult. What could happen?"

"Does the phrase 'famous last words' mean anything at all to you? Look, Marley, I'm really glad you're ready to live a little. But a good girl should never go adventuring alone. At least, not her first time, and *not* after a day like you had yesterday. Why don't you wait until I get back and we'll go adventuring together. Us girls. It'll be a blast."

Leaning back in her chair, Marley scrubbed a hand up and down her arm, feeling the excited goose bumps still. "Nope. I have to do this now. Before I wimp out and start thinking how stupid it is for an unemployed woman to consider something as potentially expensive as an adventure."

"Now. Oka-ay."

Marley smiled as she listened to her cousin stalling.

"How about this? I'll call and cancel my date and we'll just go. Today. You and me. Anywhere you want to go. I promise."

"*Sammi.* Go on your date. And don't worry about me. I'm an intelligent adult with a healthy respect for life and limb. I'll be fine. And if I'm not—" She overrode her cousin's protest. "If I'm not, you're just a phone call away. Right?"

Samantha sighed. "I don't like this." She made worried noises under her breath. "Look, I'll have my cell phone on me at all times. Call if you need me. Man, this just bites, Marley. You're supposed to play mother hen, not me."

Marley laughed again. "It'll be an eye-opening experience for you."

"That's exactly what I'm afraid of."

After hanging up, Marley turned her attention back to the computer screen. She logged onto the Internet and quickly called up her favorite travel Web site.

Las Vegas.

Las Vegas.

Las Vegas.

The words virtually pounded into her eyeballs with their brilliant colors and shock-value advertising. Apparently, it was cheap and easy to travel there. She automatically moved to click out of it, then paused. Las Vegas. *Las Vegas.* Her eyes widened. No one, but *no* one would expect her to vacation in Las Vegas. A hot spot famous for nearly every vice known to mankind could have absolutely no appeal to someone like *Marley.*

Not boring, predictable, *rational* Marley.

Fifteen minutes later, Marley had successfully exchanged her airfare and made new travel and hotel reservations.

In Las Vegas.

As she printed out the results and logged off the computer, she was trembling with nerves and elation. Marley does Vegas. Now *that* was an adventure. Heart pounding, she jumped up to pack, to secure her apartment, to—

Lose her mind? Hello? *Use your head, Marley.* What about her personal things at the office? What about—

Mentally cursing that rational voice, Marley picked up the phone again and dialed her office number. Her assistant—former assistant—would answer. Ambitious hard worker that she was, Pattie spent every Saturday at the office, though Marley had never asked it of her. "Pattie, hi. It's Marley Brentwood."

And this would be her *last* call this morning. One way or another she was blowing this burg before nightfall. Hell, she had a flight to *Vegas* to catch.

"Hi, Mar—er, Miss Brentwood." Pattie spoke hesitantly, which was odd for Pattie.

Distracted momentarily, Marley frowned. But then shook it off. Of course Pattie sounded odd. Marley had just quit her job and Pattie didn't know how to act around her former boss. "I'm sure you've heard what happened yesterday."

Pattie murmured an incoherent affirmative.

"Right. Well, I just wanted to make arrangements for the stuff in my office."

Pattie cleared her throat. "Um, I don't think— Could you hold on for a second? I'll let you talk to your father and—"

"No. I don't want to talk to him. Look, there's no rush for my stuff. I can come by in a week or so for it. Or, if it's in the way, maybe you could just box everything up and put it in storage for me?"

"Sure. I could do that. I have some time Monday.

That would be perfect." Pattie spoke in a rush, her relief apparent.

"I get it. You're swamped today." Marley nodded in understanding. "No problem. I'll give you a call later."

"Okay. Um, Miss Brent—Marley?" Pattie sounded hesitant again.

"Yes?"

"I really liked working for you. I'm sorry you're leaving. It's so hard to believe…" She stopped.

"Thanks, Pattie. That means a lot to me. Don't worry about me leaving, okay? You're going to go far in the company. I put your name in for a promotion last week, did you know?" Marley smiled. At least that much would stick.

"You did?" Pattie spoke softly.

"Sure. You deserve it."

"Um, thanks." A pause, then Pattie continued in a firm, more natural voice. "Look, Marley, I think there's something you should know—" There were some muffled thumps, muted words, and then a new voice.

"Marley." It was her father.

Her lips tightening, Marley spoke low into the phone. "I don't want to talk to you right now."

"You have to come in today. It's important." He sounded grim.

"No, I don't. I quit, remember? Goodbye." She hung up the phone, gently, then turned off the ringer.

Now. To pack. What? She paced her bedroom, pulling out drawers and throwing open the closet. How did a girl dress for an adventure? She grimaced in distaste. Not in anything Marley Brentwood owned. Businesslike, sensible clothes belonged at work. Which was where Marley spent most of her waking hours.

That was something else she'd change. But for

now, she just grabbed a selection of her most versatile mild-weather separates—tops, skirts, slacks, shoes. Anything else she needed she'd just buy when she got there.

After tossing in toiletries and other necessities, Marley snapped the lid shut on her suitcase. It was now or never. Definitely not never. She secured her apartment then hauled the suitcase out the door, pausing only to drop a stack of job-application letters in a box for overnight delivery.

As she opened her car trunk and heaved her suitcase inside, a familiar sports car slid into a parking space near hers. She groaned. *Almost.* She was almost the hell out of here—

"Marley!" Josh shut his car door and jogged over to her, his unbuttoned suit jacket flapping behind him.

Marley gave him an impatient look. "What now, Josh?"

He came to a stop a few feet away, his forehead creased in a frown. "I tried calling, but— Why the suitcase? Where are you going? I just assumed you would cancel the Denver trip."

"I did." She slammed the trunk closed and rounded the car to the driver's side. "I have a different itinerary now."

He followed. "What is it? Where are you going?"

"None of your business." She ducked into the car and slammed the door shut.

"Marley—" But she'd already turned the key in the ignition, drowning out whatever he might have thought or said. Josh was left, once again, to stare at the back end of her car as she drove away from him. The tradition was beginning to annoy him already.

As he slid into his car, he pulled out his cell phone and called his assistant. "Lynn, hi. I need you to get a phone number for me. Samantha…*Yeats,* I think. Mr. Brentwood's niece? Yes, I'll wait."

Parking neatly in his reserved space, Josh got out of the car and entered the offices of Brentwood Electronics. The place looked damn empty now that Marley was gone. He took the elevator to the top floor and rounded the corner to his office, to find both Larry Donatelli and Charles Brentwood seated and waiting for him. Not a surprise.

They'd had to table private crises in favor of critical business ones yesterday, but the subject of Marley's broken engagement couldn't be avoided forever. And in the meantime, Charles and Larry couldn't help but put two and two together.

"Good morning, gentlemen. Is there a meeting scheduled?"

Larry sat forward to glare across the desk at Josh. "Cut it out, Walker. You know damn well why we're here. Who do you think you are, telling Marley about my deal with Charles?"

"I could have your hide for that, Walker." Charles's voice was low and angry, though he stayed seated.

Josh nodded to both men. "Want my resignation, Charles?"

"Hell, no."

Josh smiled. "You're a practical man. Has it occurred to you that pragmatism isn't always a virtue?"

Charles raised a sardonic eyebrow but didn't comment.

"I think it's occurred to your daughter. And that's what concerns me. I'll be taking a leave of absence."

Charles glared at him. "At a time like this?"

"*Especially* at a time like this." Josh scowled. "I have to clean up the mess you made. I'm going after Marley."

Now Charles launched to his feet. "What do you mean going after her? Where did she go?"

"According to an unquestionable source, the airport. And that's all I'm going to tell you for now, other than I'm going to try to keep her out of trouble."

"What about the mess we have here?"

Josh glanced briefly at Larry, then spoke in an even tone. "I think you can deal with it, Charles. You owe it to Marley."

After a moment, the older man nodded. "I suppose I do. All right. You can have your leave of absence."

"Who says you're the best man to go after Marley? She's *my* fiancée, not yours." Donatelli glared at him.

"*Ex*-fiancée."

"Thanks to you."

Josh smiled without humor. "You're the one who took the deal. Not me."

"That's enough, Josh. I think we all know I'm the one who screwed up." Charles glanced at Larry. "Deal's off, by the way. I should never have made the offer."

Donatelli got up and stalked out of the office.

"So why did you do it, then?"

Charles sighed. "Hell, I don't know. I was desperate. I wanted the girl married. It's time. How the hell can I settle my affairs and retire before I know she's got someone to take care of her?"

Josh just shook his head. It would take more time than he could spare to describe what an archaic notion that was. Besides, he reflected with an inward grin, he didn't think Charles would budge in his thinking even if Josh did explain.

"But that's all beside the point. We have bigger problems on our hands now."

Grimacing, Josh nodded. "The timing's hellish, Charles." A week ago would have been better. Hell, a week ago might have solved everything, if his suspicions were correct. But now… He shook his head. "I'll pick my moment. And break everything to Marley as gently as possible."

"No." Leaning forward in his seat, Charles spoke in a low, urgent voice. "I don't want her to know about the embezzlement. Not now. She's got enough on her plate dealing with my screwups and the broken engagement."

Josh gave him a hard glance. "You want me to lie to her?"

"No. Hell, it won't take lying. She wouldn't think to even ask about this. Just don't out-and-out *tell* her about it."

"Charles—"

"I mean it, Walker. Not a word."

"Damn it, Charles, *she's* the one under suspicion. How the hell do I keep that from her? She's going to find out anyway."

The older man gave him a fierce look. "You breathe a word of this to my daughter before I okay it, and you can kiss this company goodbye. I mean it. Not one word."

Josh straightened, his temper stirring.

"Ah, don't bite at me, Josh." Charles sat back, and rubbed tiredly at his eyes. "She's my daughter. What else can I do but try to protect her from this?" He paused, frowning. "Damn it, she didn't deserve this, especially now. Just give me some time to fix the situation, find out who's really responsible, and I'll try to make things up to her later." He gave Josh a steady look. "You can give me that much, can't you?"

Reluctantly, Josh nodded.

"Still want that leave of absence to go after her?"

"Yes."

Charles looked relieved. "Good. And you'll take care of my daughter?"

"Yeah, I'll take care of her." He grimaced before continuing reluctantly. "And I won't mention the theft unless I have to. She does have enough to deal with right now."

Charles shifted and nodded. "I appreciate it. In fact, you bring her back here in one piece and I'll sign on the dotted line. Right on the spot. My word of honor."

Josh finished stacking files into his briefcase and clicked it shut. "Charles. I appreciate the gesture, but I'm not doing this for you, the company or money. I'm doing it..." He paused, considering. "Out of respect. For the value of an honest-to-God impulse."

3

WHEELING HER SUITCASE behind her, Marley navigated her way through the airport. As she approached the ticket desk, she read the posted list of flights, their destinations and arrival times. Which one was hers... *There*. Las Vegas. And it was departing...on time. In just a few short hours, she'd be in Vegas, on her very own adventure. Amazing.

Marley felt that tingling again. *Freedom*. She smiled, then stepped up to the ticket counter to collect her boarding pass.

"May I help you?" The woman gave her a brisk smile.

"I have airfare to Las Vegas." Marley frowned uncertainly for a moment. "I just bought it recently. It should be in your computer, though, right?"

"If you bought the ticket, I'm sure we have you in here."

Marley handed her the printout she'd made, plus ID.

The woman clacked away at the keyboard, blinked, then hit a single button before briefly glancing up. "You certainly did just buy your ticket. You're just showing up on my screen now."

Marley grinned and accepted her wallet back. "I didn't know I was going until just this morning."

The woman scanned the computer screen, then checked it against Marley's printout before inquiring in a near monotone. "You're aware that you pur-chased a one-way ticket?"

Marley smiled, swallowing an exuberant laugh. She'd always wanted to request a one-way ticket to someplace. It sounded so…daring. So unplanned. So…*irrational.* "Yes. A one-way ticket to Las Vegas."

The woman glanced up, her professional veneer receding. "You just bought a one-way ticket to Las Vegas. This morning."

Marley laughed. "Yes."

The woman, who looked wide-eyed for just a mo-ment, shook her head and turned back to her moni-tor. "Sorry. That just sounds like—"

"An adventure?"

"Exactly." The woman's lips twisted in a little smile, before she sobered again. "You know it's a lot cheaper to buy a round-trip than to purchase two one-way tickets."

"Yes. I just don't know when I'm returning." Or *if.*

Visualizing slot machines, glitzy shows and lux-ury hotels, Marley dreamed her way through secu-rity, then strolled off to the proper gate. Just as she was seating herself to watch planes take off, her cell phone rang. Frowning at the intrusion, she pulled the thing out of her purse and checked the number.

"Hi, Sammi. Checking up on me already?"

"Yes. And I don't like it."

Marley laughed. "I think I do."

"Where are you?"

"At the airport."

"The *airport?*"

"Mmm, hmm." Marley crossed her legs, feeling smug.

"Where are you going?"

"Las Vegas."

"*Alone?* Oh, God."

"Yes, alone. Now, calm down, Sammi. I don't intend to gamble away the family fortune." She narrowed her eyes. "As tempting as that might be. I just wanted to go someplace exciting."

"But *Las Vegas?*"

Marley closed her eyes. "Look. If you can't handle the term *adventure,* then try *vacation.* I don't know that I've ever really taken one."

After a moment of silence, Samantha sighed. "Okay, I'll buy that. A vacation. You've had a rotten few days. You're looking to relax and regroup before you take a new direction in life. So you're taking a vacation. That sounds ration—"

"Don't say it." Marley interrupted her cousin sweetly.

"Didn't even think it." Samantha's breath whooshed out over the phone line. "Okay. Where are you staying?"

Marley gave her the hotel name and phone number.

"A *casino resort,* Marley?"

"It was the best deal on the Internet." Marley grew a little exasperated. "It's just a hotel. The rating was decent."

"Okay, okay. Do you want me to come with you?"

"Will you please quit worrying about me? I am an adult."

"I know. But this is so unlike you, it's creepy. When are you coming back?"

"I'm not sure."

"Your return ticket?"

Marley grinned to herself. "Didn't buy one."

"Oh, boy."

"Sammi, *please.*" Marley spoke quietly.

"Okay. I'm sorry."

"I've listened to all the fun trips you've taken, the exciting men you've known, and I've done none of that. I don't intend to make up for all that I've missed in one trip, but I wouldn't mind getting a taste of it."

"Okay, I get it. Just call me, okay?"

"I will. Thanks, Sammi."

Marley hung up the phone. After a thoughtful moment, she switched it off. Then she turned to stare out the window. She watched a plane pick up speed down the runway and lift off, soaring higher and higher, destination unknown.

SEVERAL HOURS LATER, Marley nervously made her way into the hotel lounge. Her flight had been uneventful, the hotel amazing, her dinner…reasonable but not exactly free. Still, she refused to consider the damage to her credit card. She now considered this vacation to be no less than a rite of passage. Expenses be damned.

Setting aside thoughts of money, Marley gazed around her, eyes wide to take in the crowd, the lights, the flamboyance of it all. She sat at a small table and just gawked. Statuary in the lobby, costumed bell-hops, casinos as big as warehouses. She'd never seen anything like it. In her disoriented awe, she felt like a teenager crashing an adult party.

"Would you like to order a drink?" A young man smiled down at her.

"Um, yes. I would." She glanced around. A white wine, her usual drink of choice, just didn't seem appropriate right now. "What do you recommend?"

He cocked his head in thought.

"No, forget that." Waving a hand in a negative motion, she grabbed her courage. "Just surprise me. Something…fruity and—" she glanced around again "—a little exotic."

He laughed. "Okay."

Five minutes later, he set a pretty pink something in a big balloon glass in front of her. A thin slice of lime was curled just so and perched on the rim. It looked…frivolous…a little exotic. She smiled up at him. "Perfect."

After the waiter left, she sipped at the drink, tasting mangoes and coconut. Very sweet and no bite to it at all. She grinned ruefully. No doubt the waiter thought she looked like someone who didn't need alcohol tonight. Probably wise of him.

She frowned. Although, maybe it would be nice to do her own thinking for a change. The men around her seemed determined to run her life for her. First her father with his interference, then Larry with his duplicity and then Josh with his arrogance. Josh. So he was attracted to her. *Now*. Why?

Her little flirtation in the coffee shop all those months ago had barely registered with him. And, gee, see how his interest in her rose exponentially once he discovered who her father was? Jerk.

She sipped at her drink, remembering the sexy grin Josh had flashed at her in her apartment yesterday. Oh, it had affected her. Got all those neglected hormones in a nice little lather—and he'd never even touched her. Obviously, it had been way too long since she'd been with a man.

Such is life for a good girl, she thought, taking another sip of her fruity drink.

Just as she set the glass down again, a big-shouldered brunette with a toothy smile slid into the chair across from her. "This seat taken?"

She glanced around. There weren't many seats left. "No." She smiled reluctantly. *Rite of passage, Marley. Now is not the time to be antisocial*. That inner voice resembled Samantha at her naughtiest, which amused and irritated at the same time. Just how far was Marley willing to take this "adventure" anyway?

The brunette's eyes narrowed and she saw calculation there.

Not *that* far.

Still, it was more exciting to share a table with a man than sit alone. "Is this your first time to Las Vegas?"

"Oh, no. I make a trip out here a few times a year. Sometimes on business. Sometimes not." His smile widened. "This time's strictly for pleasure."

"That's nice." She sipped at her drink again.

After a few more minutes of small talk, she began to relax. This wasn't so hard after all. It helped to have her hands busy.

"Would you like another?"

"Hmm?" She raised her eyebrows.

"Another drink."

She glanced down. It was empty. "Oh. Yes, I would."

He grinned and signaled the waiter.

A WHOLE PLATOON of soldiers steadily marched on, over and through her head, each punishing stomp reverberating inside her skull. She couldn't even scream out a protest because they'd glued her tongue to the roof of her mouth. Right after they'd poured battery acid down her throat, and left it to pool and corrode the delicate lining of her quivering belly.

Marley groaned weakly beneath the torture, limbs sliding and flailing beneath their silken confines. The slippery material felt cool against bare legs, bare arms.

Bare torso?

Her eyelids flew open, and Marley winced. Bright morning sunshine stabbed at her dry, sandy eyes, heightening the pounding in her head. She squeezed her eyes shut again. Then, cautiously, she allowed in a sliver of light, gradually letting it widen until she was blinking at unfamiliar surroundings.

"What—?" She sat up, felt a cool breeze and

pulled the sheet up over her naked breasts. Her headache intensified.

Still clutching the sheets as though clinging to a lifeline, she gazed up in disbelief at the filmy canopy that hung over her. Then, feeling shaky, she lowered her gaze to the slippery sheets that felt so good against her skin. They were…bright red satin. She blinked. And the bed beneath her was round and set up on a platform above a gold-veined black-marble floor. A hot tub bubbled nearby.

She closed her eyes, swallowing heavily as wisps of memory emerged and coalesced into a painful— but at least familiar—whole. She was in a hotel room in Las Vegas. Alone, thank God. The last thing she remembered with clarity was a pretty drink with a curly slice of lime perched on the edge of it. Followed by a few others just like it.

Given her aching head and cotton mouth, she'd have to assume those pretty drinks were less than harmless. At that thought, a disbelieving smile tugged at her lips. In the last twenty-four hours she'd hopped on a one-way flight to Las Vegas, checked herself into a flamboyant luxury hotel, shared cocktails with a strange man, gotten drunk on exotic pink somethings and slept naked between satin sheets.

Her. Marley Brentwood. Good-girl Marley. Frigidly predictable Marley. Daddy's little nobody girl-Friday Marley. Her smile widened. Now it was hungover, unemployed, naked-under-satin-sheets-in-a-Las-Vegas-hotel, *bad*-girl Marley. And it was about time.

She chuckled weakly, then grabbed her head as pain shot through it. She winced when something on her hand got caught in a lock of hair. After untangling it, she glanced distractedly to check for damage.

And encountered what had to be *a diamond solitaire ring…with a matching band attached to it.*

With a yelp, she leaped out of bed, then danced in a wobbly circle, scrabbling with the sheet to wind it around her naked body. "Hello? Is anyone in here?" Her voice was a rusty-sounding quaver. She inventoried empty bathroom, tumbled bed and neat but uninhabited closet. Then she grabbed the crown of her head to hold it still. The headache was pounding her insane now.

But at least she was alone, she realized, sagging with relief. Then, looking down at the ring, she gave it an experimental tug.

"Oh, Lord. This can't be what it looks like. It just can't." But it sure looked like a wedding ring. What had she done?

4

"So let me get this straight, Marl." Samantha's voice, even tinny through the phone lines, registered shock and outrageous amusement. "You woke up naked in Las Vegas, with a wedding ring on your finger. And you don't know who the groom is."

"Um. Yeah?" Hearing the squeak in her own voice, Marley cleared her throat and took a breath before continuing. "That about sums it up."

Samantha coughed into the phone, a choked sound that made Marley itch to curl her fingers around her best friend's throat.

"Sammi, this is serious. Help me."

"Okay, okay. I'm sorry. It's just that it's so—so un-*Marley* of you."

"I know, I know, I know. God, what was I thinking?" Marley raked her hand through her hair, winced at the tug and glared at the offending ring again. Several strands of curly auburn had twined themselves around the prongs. They were clean strands, though; she'd taken the time to shower and pull on some clothes before telephoning Samantha for help.

When Samantha spoke again, the amusement was gone. If anything, she sounded stern. "Cut it out, Marley. You've been way overdue for a disaster like this. So you cut loose a little. Big deal. Whatever happened, we'll fix it. Okay?"

"Oh, Sammi." Her choked laugh felt more like a sob. "I'm married, I don't know to whom, and you say it's no big deal? My God, I woke up *naked!* I probably *slept* with the guy."

A sigh hissed over the line. "Okay, so maybe that part is a little scary."

Marley gestured widely. "Well, maybe just a *little*. What if he's diseased? Or a criminal? Or a career bigamist who hangs out in Vegas and collects women and marriage certificates?"

Samantha groaned. "God, Marley. Get a grip. He's probably passed out in the stairwell somewhere, as clueless as you. You'll both be embarrassed, get a quickie divorce or annulment, then each have a story to share with the grandkids someday."

"Do you think so?"

"Well, maybe it's not quite wholesome enough for the grandkids. It'd still make a good dinner-party story."

"Grandkids. God, Sammi. What if I'm pregnant?" She spoke in a hushed voice, her hand sliding to her achy stomach.

Samantha inhaled sharply. "Another worry. But we'll handle it, okay? One way or another. Now calm down, and let's take this one step at a time. First, breathe."

Marley inhaled deeply, let the breath out slowly, and focused. "Okay."

"Okay?"

"Okay. I'm here. I'm back."

"Good. Now listen. Odds are, none of those terrible things are true. Most likely, we're just looking at a misunderstanding and maybe a one-night stand." She paused. "Are you with me?"

"Yes. Okay." Marley laughed a little, but there was an edge to it. "If that's all."

Samantha groaned and chuckled softly. "Poor

Marley. You fight your way free of the leash just once and look what happens. You have more bad-girl potential than I ever dreamed."

"Stuff it, Sammi." But Marley was smiling a little now, as she knew her cousin had intended. "All right. First thing's first. I need to find the groom."

"Good plan, Marl." Samantha's admiration was too blatant to be sincere.

Marley took the receiver from her ear, glared at it, then spoke into it. "Exactly *why* did I call you again?"

"Maybe because no one else would have a clue how to handle a situation as crazy as this? Or, maybe because I'm your cousin and your best friend?"

"Or, better yet—" Marley spoke in a voice low with exaggerated warning. "Maybe it's because I have so much blackmail material to hold over *your* head. Your silence is pretty much guaranteed."

"Well, there is that."

Marley heard a familiar rasping sound that was undoubtedly— "In the midst of my crisis, are you *filing your nails?*"

"It helps me think. Now, about finding your groom. What have you done so far?"

Marley grimaced and tugged at her hair again. With her unadorned right hand this time. "Well, no one's in the room with me. And no one's hanging out in the hallway."

"You need to venture a little farther then."

Marley gasped. "The toothy brunette. It has to be him." She squeezed the bridge of her nose between thumb and forefinger. "Cards. He was showing me how to cheat at cards. Oh, Lord."

Samantha whistled. "Cheating at cards. This just keeps getting better."

"Please, Sammi."

"Okay, okay. So you think it might be him?"

"He's the last guy I remember."

"Okay, start there." Samantha spoke decisively. "He's probably staying at the hotel. Get his room number."

Marley mumbled into the phone.

"What?"

"I don't know his name, okay?" Pride in her adventure was rapidly succumbing to sheer humiliation.

There was silence...then a suspicious snorting sound.

"You are not—I repeat—*not* laughing at me. Are you."

"N-no."

Marley sighed. "Okay, get it out of your system. I need you clearheaded."

Samantha snorted again and covered the phone, but Marley could hear laughter. She deserved it. After all the lectures she'd read Sammi over the years, she really had this coming. Otherwise, she'd be hanging up the phone right about now.

"Are you done yet?"

"Yes. Okay, I'm done. Hold on a sec—I need to get something." Marley heard rummaging, more giggles, and then Samantha was back. "Okay. So you need to find out this guy's name. Start questioning your waiter, the hotel staff, the desk clerk, maybe some of your near neighbors."

Marley laughed, her stomach tightening. "I guess I could just ask if they've seen my groom anywhere? And when they ask for a description, I'll just smile vacantly and say their guess is as good as the bride's?"

"Subtlety, Marley. Come on, you're smarter than this. Use some of that boardroom savvy in your personal life."

"You mean be vague?" Marley smiled viciously.

Samantha laughed. "Shut up. You're a whiz at your job."

"I'm unemployed."

"Temporarily."

"I worked for my father."

"He was damn lucky to have you."

Marley sighed. "I love you. You have a smart mouth and you live a dangerous life I think I'd rather just dream about. But you're always there for me. I owe you."

"Same goes, Marl. Now, I want you to be honest. Do you need money?" Samantha, for all her wild ways, would offer a friend the shirt off her back if necessary.

"No, I'm okay for now. Us cautious types are famous for our little nest eggs. But thanks."

"And the head. You must have one hell of a hangover."

Marley just closed her eyes and groaned an affirmative.

"Take some aspirin and drink a lot of water."

"Right." Water. Aspirin. Her stomach just heaved at the thought. Maybe later.

"Good. Go look for your groom, then, and call me tonight." Samantha hung up.

Marley replaced the receiver, dread threatening to overwhelm her. She took a deep breath, did an exaggerated about-face, then marched to the door.

At the last second, she detoured to the mirror, to check out the damage from last night's binge and this morning's anxiety. Circles, bloodshot eyes, pale skin, wild hair...terrifying. She sighed, ran a damp comb through her curls, applied lipstick, then surveyed again. At least she wouldn't scare the guy. Well, maybe not at first.

Marley set off to find her groom.

SEATED IN A GROUPING of chairs with an unobstructed view of elevators and stairs, Josh stared moodily ahead of him. The elevator doors opened yet again. A young couple wrapped up in each other spilled out, followed by an older woman with a straw bag and an attitude, and then, finally, a slender woman with a pale face and nervous golden eyes. She raked a hand through shoulder-length auburn curls and glanced warily around the lobby before heading to the registration desk.

Her gaze might have been wary, but her stride was no-nonsense. And her body, if she'd only acknowledge it, was an intriguing display of restrained sensuality. Josh smiled slightly. His gaze glided down to the long, long legs, graceful in spite of themselves beneath a straight skirt and sensible cotton sweater. Navy pumps clicked rhythmically across the expanse of black marble.

When she reached the desk, she turned her back to him, one hip jutting out slightly as she shifted her weight. She gestured elegantly with slender hands. The young desk clerk frowned in puzzlement before shrugging and pointing across the lobby.

She turned to follow the direction he was pointing and seemed to freeze in place. Without turning her head, she spoke briefly then moved in the direction she was looking.

Josh studied the crowd, his gaze lighting on a broad-shouldered guy with dark brown hair and a smile that belonged in a toothpaste ad. He frowned, his mood lowering even more.

WITH HESITANT STEPS, Marley approached the man the clerk had indicated. Squinting slightly, she grew more agitated and yet more confident with each step. It was him, the one she remembered from last night. She halted a few steps away from him. "Hi."

"Hi, beautiful." He parted his lips only slightly in a smile so intimate it made her stomach churn.

"Hi. Are you…enjoying Las Vegas?" *Oh, witty, Marley. So witty.*

His smile widened. "Very much. Thanks to you."

"Thanks to—" *Oh, God. Steady, Marley.* She licked her lips.

He shifted to a cockier stance, his expression equally suggestive as he studied her mouth.

"Last night—"

"Was great. How about a repeat performance tonight?"

"What?" Her pitch and tone verged on shrill.

His smile faltered.

Attempting a smile, she lowered her voice. "A repeat of…which performance?"

"Yours." His eyelids drooped and he smirked knowingly.

Marley wished for a small, dark place in which to hide. For a year maybe. "Oh, boy." The words came out in a shaky whisper.

He laughed, not unsympathetically. "Too many rum punches?"

"*Rum* punches— Oh, well that figures." She squeezed her eyes shut. "Yes, I think I had my share. I'll be avoiding those from now on."

"Bummer. Does that mean you won't sing anymore, either?"

"Sing?" Her voice rose in disbelief. "*Sing?* I don't sing."

The group behind him laughed. One man, who looked as if he'd already had his share of rum punches this morning, raised his voice over the others. "We know you don't sing. The whole damn lounge knows you can't sing."

Marley covered her face. Great. She shook her head. "Don't worry. I won't torture you with a repeat performance." Reluctantly, she dropped her hands to her sides and faced the brunette. "Can I talk to you alone for a minute?"

He raised a teasing eyebrow. "Oh, so now you

have time for me. Couldn't get you alone for a minute last night."

She stared. "Not at all?"

"Nope." He gave her a cajoling grin. "But I'm damn glad you came by to make up for that. How about we—"

"Um—" Stepping back with a nervous laugh, she tugged on a curl while she scrambled for a mental foothold. "Actually, I've been trying to find a friend. Of mine. He… Well, he's a little hard to describe, and—"

His grin grew lopsided. "Just my luck. Guess Bran caught you after all, huh?"

Bran. Did she remember a Bran? Probably short for Brandon…? Oh, Lord, this was ludicrous. A woman could only call upon so much acting skill. She forced a beguiling grin. "Who says I need to be caught?" She tucked her left hand discreetly behind her back. "I just wanted to have a word with…Bran. Do you happen to know where he is?"

The guy shrugged. "Yeah, I just passed him. He was in the lounge, over there." He grimaced. "Probably partying already. Wouldn't be surprised if he's passed out by noon."

At the idea of drinking anything even remotely resembling— Her stomach turned over. She swallowed hard. "Thanks. Any idea which table…"

"Oh, he's at the bar. You couldn't miss him if you tried. That's got to be the ugliest Hawaiian shirt I've ever seen."

"Thanks. Um, nice meeting you—" She blinked. *Still no name.* "—last night." She gave an awkward half wave, ignored the resulting laughter and jeers from his friends, then set off for the lounge. Veering right at the corner, if she recalled correctly. She did.

Entering the lounge, she glanced around cautiously before she found the bar. It was disturbingly familiar. She winced, then heard this horrible moaning sound…wailing?…a man *singing*? If any music had actually been playing, she might have understood, but—

"Na-na-nah Lo-laaah…and, um, the sssha-sha…" The man waved his beer around, sloshing some across his—yes—ugly Hawaiian shirt, before he caught sight of her and stopped mutilating Manilow.

"Well, holy crap. Ginger, baby! Come *here*, darlin'. I've missed you somethin' awful."

Ginger? A disguise? Well, that would be the first smart thing she'd done last night, but—

"Come to Fred, baby. You are one hot number. From dancing queen by night to red-hot businesswoman by day. Whatcha got on under that prissy little skirt, darlin'?"

He snagged her hand, tugged until she twirled and slammed up against his chest, then he spun her back out again. She stumbled over a stool, and he pulled her upright, back into his arms for a clumsy waltz. She grabbed handfuls of his shirt and skidded to a nauseous stop. "Er…Fred. Bran? Could we stop for a second? I'm a little dizzy."

He laughed uproariously. "Hey, I tried to warn you. Don't do shots after rum punch. That's just too damn much for anyone. Tequila on top of rum? Yow."

"Tequila?"

"Oh, yeah. But I gotta admit you do know your way around a lime. Oooh, baby." He did a slurpy imitation of a woman sucking citrus.

Her stomach lurched again. "Right." Forcing a weak laugh, she tried to look helpless and appealing. "Could we sit? And talk?"

He gave a disappointed sigh. "It's a shame to sit when we could be dancin'. Floor's not even crowded today. Won't have to boost you onto the table again like last night."

"Table? As in *dancing on?"* She felt like a parrot. A helpless, foolish female one.

"Well, only when you weren't dancing on the bar. Bar's higher. We could all see and cheer you on up there. But then you slipped and of course the bartender got a little pissed. So we switched to tables after that."

Table dancing. *Don't think about it, Marley.* It could be worse. Still— "I thought I just sang. A lot."

He grinned. "You sang all right. But they made you stop, so you said if a woman can't sing, she's damn well gotta dance. No argument from me, darlin', and that's exactly what I told you. Your singing sucks, but the dancing..." He shook his head, grinning. "Never woulda guessed a classy woman like you would know some dirty-dancin' moves."

"Oh." *Eeeeew.*

He scowled. "Too bad whatsisface stopped us before we could get going. I had plans for later. You'd'a liked 'em." He leered. "'S why I'm so damn glad to see you now. Hell, I'll even let you take your shirt off this time like you wanted to last night."

She closed her eyes on a silent groan. Surely not. But she remembered seeing posters. Revue dancers. Talented, beautiful women with the nerve to dance half-naked on a stage. They'd seemed so daring. You could bet no one ran *their* lives for them... Okay, she could follow her own drunken thought processes, but still, the topless bit...*really* not her style.

Focus. Hawaiian-shirt man was not her man, but this other guy, the one who halted the risqué dancing— "I think I'll pass, thanks. But about the guy, um, *whatsisface*...the one who stopped the—*dancing?"* On bars. Nearly shirtless. Oh, God.

"Aw, don't worry about it." Obviously reacting to her wince, he patted her shoulder clumsily, a big, bearlike gesture that knocked her off balance. "A girl should be allowed to let loose once in a while. And he's not here to stop you this time."

She gritted her teeth, resisting the urge to fold her arms across the breasts he stared at so avidly, and fought for patience. "He *who*?"

The guy scowled. "Manager."

Her hopes fell, as did her dignity. As though she had any left. "I got kicked out?"

He shook his head. "Volunteered."

It just got worse and worse. "For?"

"They had this auction going later."

She closed her eyes. "Please tell me I was the auctioneer or a helper of some kind?" She was going to be sick soon.

He laughed uproariously. "No, baby. Not when grown men would pay cold, hard cash for somethin' as hot as you. Nope, you were *merchandise*."

"For sale?" Her voice was faint.

"Well, in a manner of speaking." He belched, then held up an index finger, looking a little panicked all of a sudden. "Er, jussgonnahaftascusemeforminit—" He barreled out of the lounge, eyes on a rest-room sign.

"But wait—" She'd gotten more information out of the drunk than anyone so far. No way was she letting him out of her sight.

A hand snagged her elbow. "Let him go, ma'am. Trust me."

She glanced back impatiently. "I have to…" Then she stared. "I remember you."

He smiled, a very nice smile. "The mystery-drink lady. How'd you like the rum punch? It's our specialty." He tucked a bar rag into his back pocket.

"It was good." The first one really was. And she couldn't hold it against the guy for just doing what she'd asked. He was a waiter, possibly a bartender— but not a baby-sitter.

His smile faded. "Although maybe you shouldn't

have followed up with the dancing, tequila and cigars."

"Cigars, too, huh?" She was growing numb to it. The revelations. There were so many, after all.

"Hey, don't worry about it. It was only just the one cigar. You had the sense to quit after a puff or two. It's an acquired taste." He smiled.

"Just a puff or two. Well, if that's all."

He nodded encouragingly, obviously missing the irony in her tone, due to the hoarseness of her voice.

"So, how about that auction last night..." She let her words trail off, raising an eyebrow hopefully.

He laughed. "Funniest damned thing I've seen in a while. I thought there was going to be a knock-down, drag-out fight."

"Oh, yeah?" She cleared her throat, hoping to brazen her way to more information, heaven help her. "These auctions get pretty wild..."

He shook his head, still chuckling. "Yeah, but the fights are usually in the audience. How's the head doing, anyway?"

Her hangover. "Oh, been better."

"She really corked you one good." He shrugged. "Good thing we pulled her off you before any real damage was done, but I think you could've taken her. She's big but you're in better shape." He gave her legs an admiring glance.

Bar brawl. She'd been in a bar brawl. My, how far the prissy had fallen. "I think she started it." She must have. Or, at this rate, maybe not—

"Well, hell. It's not your fault the guy kept bidding on you instead of her. You cost him a lot of dough, too, but I guess he was determined to have you." The bartender shrugged. "It was just dumb luck that Fiona had her eye on *him*."

Marley stared. Sometimes there just were no words. She licked her lips carefully. "Him...who?"

"You know. The guy who bought you. Gold chain around his neck? Something sparkly?"

She nodded vaguely, hoping he'd mistake the gesture for recognition.

"Oh, I get it." The bartender smiled in sudden comprehension. "He's your boyfriend, right? Well, that explains it. Nobody pays that much for a woman unless—" He cleared his throat, obviously biting back words and a chuckle.

But Marley was pretty sure she could fill in that blank. No man paid that much money for a woman unless she was already his and/or he expected to get laid. This could be her groom.

Talk about irony. She went from dumping a fiancé her father purchased for her, to getting bought by her current husband. Unnamed, at that. Money and marriage. Who would have thought they'd be so closely related in this day and age?

"Yeah, anyway. It was quite the spectacle."

"I'll bet." She cleared her throat: "I'm sorry for any trouble I caused last night."

He waved off her apology with a grin. "It was pure entertainment. You were quite the crowd pleaser. Well, except for the singing." He shrugged apologetically.

She just closed her eyes and nodded. "Right. No singing." Singing bad.

"And, if you'd take some advice…"

"Yes?" She was almost afraid to hear it.

"I'd dump that guy if I were you. I think you drank half those tequila shots just because he wouldn't leave you the hell alone or stop telling you what to do. He just kept hovering so you kept pounding them back."

An opening. "Actually, I've been looking for him. Probably to dump him, like you suggested. Have you seen him lately?"

He flicked a thumb past his shoulder. "Sure. But maybe have some pity on the guy before you send him on his way. Tell him to lose the suits and long pants. Guy should get himself some shorts. Air-conditioning or no air-conditioning, this is still the desert." He glanced over his shoulder. "At least he lost the jacket this time. Made me sweat last night just to look at him."

"No suits in the desert. Got it." She followed the thumb and saw a rail-thin, dour-looking man folded up behind a table across the aisle. In pin-striped slacks and shirt, he still looked warm, though he'd draped the suit jacket over the back of his chair. He was frowning into a newspaper as she approached him.

Could it be him? Her husband? This was getting old. Maybe she should just outright ask the man if they'd exchanged vows. It wasn't as if she had any pride left to preserve.

"Hi."

The man glanced up at her blankly.

She gave him a determined smile. "Do I know you?"

"Excuse me?" He darted a nervous glance around.

Beyond humiliation, she gave an impatient sigh. "Did we get married last night?"

He just goggled at her, his mouth opening and closing speechlessly.

Thank God. "Never mind. It was a trick question."

He stared, a little dazedly.

She glanced back at the waiter, who was grinning hugely. He discreetly pointed toward a group of chairs near the elevators.

Right. She responded with a weak smile and nod, then turned in the direction he'd pointed. *Don't think about it, don't think about it, don't think about it.* Her mind carefully blank, she obediently headed toward the grouping of chairs. Saw a guy with long, loose pants. Something sparkly around his neck...

FROM A FEW TABLES OVER, Josh watched Marley walk toward some chairs he'd vacated to try to listen in on her conversation. Where was she going now? He studied the group and saw her approach a tall, blond man who was eyeing her steadily.

She bit down on her lower lip as she closed the distance between her and the man. Josh frowned. Enough of this. The suspense was killing him. He surged to his feet.

SLOWLY APPROACHING the group of chairs, Marley kept her gaze trained on a big blond man with a glittering chain around his neck. Dog tags? Could be military? As she closed the distance between them, she realized it was just a medallion on the chain. It glittered, kind of.

Okay, this might not be so bad. He seemed normal, probably reasonable. Even good-looking in a slick, untrustworthy way. She tried a smile. "Hi."

He returned the smile, his eyes intimate. "Hi."

"Look, this might sound strange, but—"

"Not at all." His voice was husky as he stood up and moved in closer, his interest heightened. "I've been waiting for you."

She swallowed heavily and her smile faltered. All fingers had, in the end, pointed to this guy. It was probably him. Her groom. Oh, God. The singing and dancing and drinking were all unsettling but bearable. But this...

She'd deal. She had to. Deliberately, she lifted her chin. "I'm sorry to keep you waiting, then."

"It was worth every minute, beautiful."

Okay, so he wasn't exactly original. "Thanks. Could we find someplace to talk?"

"Perfect."

Unless she was very much mistaken, that full

head of blond hair was somebody else's. Why did men try to pull off toupees, anyway? Honestly, blatantly bald, paired with a wealth of confidence, did more for a man than a rug ever could.

She sighed, realizing she was distracting herself from the real cause of her distress. Ignore the drinking and dancing and singing and lineup of male encounters. None of that was life-altering. The wedding ring, however…

Just get the annulment, or—she winced—divorce if it was too late for an annulment. *Keep the goal in sight, Marl.*

In the meantime, she gently shrugged his hand off her shoulder and picked up speed to avoid further such contact. Just as she was approaching an unoccupied table, she felt a hand at her elbow. She turned with a careful, tight smile, expecting the blonde's cheesy grin to imply any number of intimacies they might have shared.

Her smile fled when she encountered a familiar pair of green eyes, hard and unsmiling as they met hers. "*Josh.* What are you doing here?" Talk about a clashing of worlds. *Hello, reality, meet insanity. Welcome to the chaos that is my life.* Glancing back at the blonde, she slid her left hand behind her back, and tried to maintain her composure.

"I'm just checking up on you." He eyed her with a frown.

She pulled her arm free. "You mean you followed me."

"I had to make sure you were okay."

"I'm fine. Now go away."

"Be reasonable, Marley. I was worried about you. Your father is, too."

She smiled tightly. "So he sent you. His top barracuda. Well, you've seen me. I'm fine. Now you can leave."

"I don't think so. We need to talk."

The unlikely blonde stepped forward with a glare. "I don't think the lady has anything to say to you, Jack."

Josh raised an eyebrow at the "Jack." "Stay out of this."

"If she doesn't want to talk to you, she doesn't want to talk to you." The blonde puffed out his chest. "If you have a problem with that, maybe you and I ought to take this outside."

Marley stepped between them, feeling the urge to knock their chauvinistic heads together. "Enough. Josh, leave. And you—" She paused awkwardly, again lacking a name for a guy who could be her husband. What a farce. She just hated to play it out in front of anyone from the real world. "Please, Josh, just go. I don't need interference from you or my father right now."

Josh's lips tightened, but he stepped back so the couple could sit. Eyeing them still, he chose a table nearby and slid into a chair. Marley glared but decided to ignore him for now.

She turned to her companion with a determined smile. "So."

He smiled back at her and opened his mouth to respond, but his words were lost in the screech of Josh's chair sliding back from his table. The couple watched as Josh stood and reached across another table, smiled at an older woman, and snagged a discarded newspaper. He dropped back into his chair. As Marley continued to watch, he flipped the paper open, noisily turning pages and folding, then met her eyes with an inquiring smile.

Marley glared, then turned in her seat so her back was to the aggravating man. She forced a smile. "So, where were we?"

"I believe we were getting to know each other better."

Marley laughed wryly. "Right. It's about time, I guess."

"Can't argue with that." He reached across the table, snagged her unwilling hand, and began playing with her fingers.

A crackling noise distracted her attention. Marley glanced over her shoulder to see Josh folding and refolding his paper. Setting one section of it aside, he opened the next and raised an eyebrow at her. A faint smile, implying infinite patience, still curved his firm mouth.

"Should we move?" the as-yet-nameless man asked her, an edge creeping into his voice.

"No." She sighed. "He'd just follow anyway." She tugged her hand free, then laced her fingers together in a frustrated, white-knuckled fist. Civilized speech was almost beyond her at this point, so why mince words? "How about we just skip all of the preliminary stuff, okay? Last night... Well, last night was a big mistake. It shouldn't have happened."

He stared blankly at her.

Hello? Maybe if she pounded him on the head he'd start spewing information for her? Her discomfort growing, she pounded her fisted hands lightly against the edge of the table. "Look. I'm sure you're a nice man, but I had way too much to drink last night."

"Hey, so you didn't have a good time last night. Can't say I didn't warn you."

Nonplussed, Marley stared for a moment. From all accounts, she'd had way too *much* fun last night, not too little. Still... "You say you warned me?"

The man shrugged. "Sure." He leaned forward. "So, now that the spousal unit's out of the way, maybe *I* can show you a good time. We could go to this other casino downtown."

Marley leaned forward in her chair, ignoring the man's invitation altogether. "'*Spousal* unit?'"

The blonde shrugged, a little impatient now. "You know. Boyfriend or husband or whatever? The guy from last night."

"*Which* guy?" Her voice lowered to a whisper but, gradually, the truth was dawning on her. And it wasn't a nice truth.

The blonde gestured obliquely. "Him. Auction guy. Asshole outbid me. And there I was, willing to put down a lot of cash on you—singing or no singing."

Ignoring the last whining comment, she slowly turned her gaze in the direction he had pointed.

"Hell, if I'd won something at blackjack last night, he'd never have taken me, but..."

She ignored his patter, just stared at her worst nightmare. Hawaiian-shirt guy would have been preferable. Even the suit. Hell, even the mimbo sitting across from her. *Anyone* else.

But Josh just stared back at her, a faint, patient smile on his lips as he uncrossed his legs. Long pants with very sharp creases. Possibly suit pants... She raised her gaze, noticed the faint glitter of gold at the open collar of his shirt. A thin gold chain.

"Oh, *God* no." She pushed her chair back, swallowing convulsively.

The blonde sat back and gave her a cautious look. "What? You're not going to be sick, are you?"

She certainly felt like it, but she ignored the blonde altogether as she carefully made her way to the nearby table. She looked down at Josh.

His smile was calm.

"You?"

Their eyes met and then, slowly, inevitably, drifted down to the flash of gold on her left hand. She glanced up.

He raised his eyebrows. "Does this mean you're ready for that talk now?"

5

"You? This is *your* ring?" Marley stared at Josh dazedly.

When she listed dizzily to the side, he grabbed her hand and gently nudged her into a chair.

"I don't believe this." She raised a trembling hand to her temple. "I think I'm going to be sick."

"That's it. I'm outta here." The blonde, who'd risen to his feet when Marley left his table, held up both hands in surrender. "She's all yours, Jack." With a hurried salute, the man all but sprinted away from threatened illness.

Marley didn't spare the blonde a glance. Her attention was focused entirely on Josh. She spoke in a hoarse whisper. "I married *you*? Of all people? How many drinks did I *have*?"

He stilled for a moment. "You don't remember?"

Weakly, she just shook her head.

"Anything?" His lips twitched. "Not even Elvis?"

She moaned and hugged her middle. "No. I remember nothing beyond a pretty pink drink with a lime slice. Oh, God. No more limes."

"The rum punch." He said the words musingly, studying her.

"Of course it was that stupid rum punch. And probably some of the tequila that supposedly followed it. Why else would I marry my father's *peon*?" She opened her eyes wide, trying to emphasize the horror of her situation.

Drinking, dancing, singing, a single rebellious—
what had she been thinking?—cigar. A bar brawl.
She could understand all of it. But this? Why on earth
would she have married Josh, of all people? Surely
there didn't exist enough alcohol in all of Sin City to
convince her to do that.

He gave her a harmless smile. "Why, Marley. If I
didn't know any better, I'd think you hadn't fallen
madly in love with me last night."

"Oh, God." She closed her eyes, taking deep,
shaky breaths.

"I mean, you did get into a fight over me with another woman." He smiled, slow and insinuating.

She groaned. "Okay, that's it for me. No more adventures. I can't be trusted with them."

He tipped his head back and laughed.

So, apparently, she was entertaining again. How
nice for him. Her temper overriding sense, she gave
him an accusing look. " I can't believe I married you
last night. Of all people. I'd have to be on something
illegal to allow that to happen. You know, one of
those horrible knockout drugs?" She gave him a vicious look. "The kind that destroy the female's con-
scious ability to resist a man, no matter how
repulsive he is?"

"I don't know how much more of this my ego can
take. I didn't put anything in your drink. You just—
apparently—put way too many drinks inside of
you." He shrugged. "Maybe I had a few too many,
too. But, unlike you, I *do* remember last night."

He kept his gaze on her, infuriating and intent,
while she felt the blood drain from her cheeks and
the world tilt just a bit. As she watched, he let a smile
drift across his lips, let his gaze fall to the curve of
her mouth. "I remember every minute of it."

She swallowed hard. And yet again. It was a losing battle.

He frowned. "Marley?"

She was off like a shot, and through the doors of the rest room before he could ask if she was okay. Josh was left to stare after her in mingled amusement and guilt. He hadn't meant to push her over the edge, just needle her a little. She had given his ego some hefty shoves, and after a point, it was hard not to nudge back.

With a grimace, Josh resumed his seat to wait for her. Despite everything, he couldn't deny the dark humor of the situation. Apparently, the very idea of exchanging vows with him—making love with him—made the woman physically ill.

He smiled wryly.

Not the most optimistic way to start a marriage.

INSIDE THE REST ROOM, Marley leaned weakly against the stall door, having worshiped porcelain in earnest. A seriously appropriate finale to her morning of discovery. *God.* Shoving away from the door, she went to rinse out her mouth—and try to reclaim whatever brain cells she hadn't destroyed the night before.

She was married. To *Josh.*

"Oh, no. Not for long. Hell, if I can drink myself to the point of mindlessness and get married all in one night, then a simple morning-after divorce should be a snap."

With new purpose, she glared at the diamond manacled onto her finger and gave it a good yank. It resisted. Oh, no. She'd get the damn wedding band off if she had to take off her finger to do it.

Still, after ten minutes of tugging and running water over the ring, she succeeded only in making her finger sore and swollen. "So I'll find a damn jeweler to *cut* it off."

The door opened behind her. "Marley?"

She spun around, then grabbed the edge of the sink when the world seemed to shift. She closed her eyes for a steadying moment, then opened them. Good grief, but the man had nerve. "What are you *doing* in here? This is the ladies' room."

Josh glanced quickly around and behind him, apparently saw no one to object, then walked boldly into no-man's land. "You were taking too long. I was worried about you."

"Well, I'm fine. Go away." The man was forever in the vicinity of her most humiliating moments. *"Go."*

"Only if you come with me. I want to keep an eye on you. And I think we need to discuss some things."

He had a point. She sighed, turned to follow him, then stopped. "You go on ahead. I'll be out in a minute." She glared. "No way am I walking out of the *ladies'* room with you."

He grinned. "Fine. I'll face the mob without your support. But if you're not out in two minutes, I'm coming in after you, whether the place is empty or not."

And he would, too. She watched in mute disgust as the man left. Turning back to the mirror, she tried to rub some color back into her pasty cheeks. She finger-combed her flattened hair, then turned to leave, reluctance warring with resolve.

Josh had moved to a table closer to the rest rooms, no doubt so he could thwart any escape attempts. Fuming silently, she joined him at the table.

"Feeling better?"

"Somewhat. Thank you." She had to force the words out.

He laughed.

She glared. "Is something funny?"

"Just the way you can mind your p's and q's when you'd much rather see me take a flying leap into the Grand Canyon."

"So I'm civilized. That's more than you can say, taking advantage of an obviously intoxicated woman."

His eyebrows rose in disbelief. "So now this situation is *my* fault?"

"No, not entirely. I'm pretty sure you didn't pour *all* of those drinks down my throat. But you must have known I was in no condition to take vows of *matrimony*, for heaven's sake. My God, Josh, I was drunk out of my mind last night. How *could* you?"

"So you regret last night?"

"You're only *just* beginning to realize this?"

He glanced at her hand. "You're still wearing my ring."

"Only because I can't get the blasted thing off." She bit off the words and buried her hand in her lap. "Now my finger's so swollen I'll never get it off."

He frowned. "Let me see."

Reluctantly, she drew her hand from her lap and extended it. He cupped her wrist and gently manipulated her ring finger. "Ouch. I think the circulation's okay, though. Leave it alone for a while and dunk it in some ice water before you try again."

She expelled her breath on a huff. "I know that much, Einstein. Meanwhile, I'm stuck wearing this damn ring of yours. How did I get myself into this?"

He grinned crookedly. "So you do accept part of the blame?"

She sighed in defeat. "Sure. Drinking. Singing. Table dancing. Bar brawls. Why would marriage be outside the realm of last night's possibilities?" Her shamelessness apparently knew no bounds. "Look, what's done is done. Let's just get this mess straightened out so we can move on with our lives."

"Okay. So, shall we live at your place or mine? I vote for mine. I've seen your place and mine is bigger. Plus, I have covered parking."

She groaned. "By mess, I mean *marriage,* you idiot. I want a divorce or an annulment or whatever it takes to make last night null and void."

"All of last night?"

Her gaze wobbled, shied away from the intimate gleam in his. "Every bit of it that involved *you.*"

"Ah, Marley. And here I thought you were finally ready to take some chances in life. Even be just a little...*irrational* at times. But you're still afraid, aren't you? Can't you allow yourself the occasional impulse?"

"Impulse?" She all but shrieked the word then lowered her voice to a more moderate, if quivering, pitch. "An impulse is buying ice cream when it's not on the shopping list. Or taking the long way home from work so you can feed the ducks."

"Hmm." He smiled lazily at her. "That sounds nice."

"Or even drinking a little too much and making a fool of yourself in a town where no one knows you." She tightened her hands into fists, the gold band hard and biting and unfamiliar against her fingers. "It's okay to be impulsive, even a little unwise sometimes when the occasion calls for it. But *this?*" She thrust her fist beneath his nose, the hated diamond glittering from her ring finger. "Marrying a man I don't even *like,* much less *love?* That qualifies as temporary *insanity.*"

"Youch. I guess this means the honeymoon's over?"

"Oooh. You're impossible." She slid her chair back, prepared to march up to her room and call an attorney. As she got up, though, her knees buckled.

Josh grabbed her arm to steady her. "Whoa. Okay, Marley. Take it easy. Why don't you just sit back down and we'll *calmly* discuss our circumstances. I promise. Okay?"

Seeing the teasing light fade from his eyes, Marley let him ease her back into her chair.

Josh eyed her appraisingly. "Don't move. I'll be back."

At her grudging nod—she'd pass out if she stood up anyway—he rose to his feet and went into a small shop nearby. A few moments later, he returned and set a tall plastic bottle on the table in front of her.

"Drink it." He smiled wryly. "You're dehydrated. Water will make you feel better and kill that monster headache."

Her mouth as dry as the arid landscape outdoors, Marley didn't argue. She opened the bottle and downed a third of its contents.

"Better?" Josh raised an eyebrow, his expression indulgent for the moment.

"Yes. Thank you." She glanced up and then away, feeling uncomfortable now. This caring version of Josh was a stranger, as far as she was concerned. For the most part anyway. He'd been almost kind one other time, at her apartment when he'd come to check on her and offer help. She frowned, confused.

"Water does the trick most of the time." He smiled. "Keep that in mind for future binges."

She glared but didn't comment, just continued drinking the water. It *was* helping. But she never intended to require the remedy again.

Overwhelmed suddenly by the consequences of last night's folly, she spoke up quietly. "Josh?"

"Hmm?" He was doing it again, that patient watching that was so unnerving.

"Last night…" Oh, Lord, could she ask—?

"Yes?" His gaze sharpened.

"Like I said, I don't really remember much, except, well, the rum drinks." She swallowed heavily. "After that, it's kind of a blur." She continued in a low voice. "I've run into people. And they've told me things. Disturbing things. I understand there was some… singing. But I don't remember that, either."

His mouth twitched. "You really can't sing worth a damn, you know. The enthusiasm is there, but the talent?" He just shook his head, eyes twinkling.

She gave in to her impatience. "So I can't sing. I can't sing, I can't sing, I can't sing."

His smile widened. "Dancing, however, you do very well."

She groaned. "Fine. Whatever. I was an idiot. Can we get past all that now?" He shrugged and she smiled grimly. "Good. Now tell me how I ended up with this stupid ring on my finger."

He started to speak, and when she gritted her teeth and braced for the worst, he stopped. Then he just studied her for a silent moment. "Well, damn. The whole idea is that repulsive to you? Marrying me? Sharing a bed with me?" He slid his hand across the table until his fingertips brushed hers.

She fidgeted in her chair, trying to blink away the sensory image of herself sliding naked between satin sheets. With Josh. It wouldn't go away. She felt heat flooding her body, intensifying and then pooling in a disturbing mass of need in the pit of her belly. *Get a grip, Marley.* She stiffened her spine and recrossed her legs, intending to zing him with the best insult she could manage.

But the honest disappointment in his eyes stole the pleasure from any stinging remark she might have made. She sighed. "No. Not repulsive. Exactly. Just…not something I would choose for myself right now." The words felt stilted, insufficient. A little dishonest even.

She remembered, with unease, their encounter at her apartment, when he'd effortlessly scrambled her senses. *Again.* The man had an effect on her, and it was anything but revulsion. Not that *that* should be a concern right now. Her only priority now was to undo whatever madness she'd created last night—

"I don't find it repulsive, either."

She glanced up, startled and reluctantly curious.

His eyes had darkened and his voice lowered. "Far from it, in fact. You have a beautiful body. And that convoluted mind of yours." He shook his head, a slow smile curving his mouth. "They've been giving me fits for weeks now. Months even."

"Months?" The one word was all she could force past the constricted muscles of her throat. Then reason caught up to her. And realization. "Oh, my God. Are you actually *hitting* on me now? Of all times?" Her voice wobbled and she felt the onset of hysterical laughter. She squelched it.

He only studied her face with a curious smile. "Why not? You've fascinated me for a hell of a long time. I'm tired of waiting for the right moment." He slid his hand closer, touched her fingertips. "I've tried to get to know you better, but you always push me away. Never could figure out why, until I started understanding how things were between you and your father." Hard fingertips brushed the tender skin between her fingers as he laced their hands together.

The touch felt familiar, dislodging a wisp of memory. Mostly a blur, but some detail. Mostly sensory. She glanced down at their linked hands, olive skin caressing paler flesh, and could easily visualize it on a larger scale. Goose bumps pricked the skin on the back of her neck. Helpless to resist the memory, she experienced a visceral recollection of his arm supporting her naked back, both sliding against satin sheets. She felt as breathless now as she had at that moment—

And the memory faded into darkness. She raised her eyes to meet his watchful gaze. "I remember."

"Do you?"

"A little. I remember—" She swallowed. "Something."

"What? The auction?" His lips twitched.

Recalling a whirl of laughter and an auctioneer's tongue-twisting patter…angry feminine voice…she grimaced and nodded. "A little." Then she tried to recall the other again, felt warm, wished she could recapture…but then it faded. She felt a strange loss. What had she missed?

He raised an eyebrow, encouraging her to continue.

"I—" She cleared her throat and tried to reclaim her hand. He squeezed it, a coaxing grip that asked to remain. She left her hand where it was. "In my room. You were holding me."

He waited, his gaze intent and his hand warm on hers.

She shook her head, frustrated. She'd almost captured it. Parts of everything—except the most important ones. The lasting ones. "That's all I remember. Nothing else. I don't remember vows or the ring or—"

"Or?"

She shook her head helplessly. "Or anything else." The unspoken reference to any lovemaking that might have occurred afterward was as obvious as the nearly nude statue hovering nearby. And as hot as the look Josh was giving her right now.

"That's all? Huh. I wonder if I should be offended."

She glanced away, saw the bottled water and made a desperate grab for it with her free hand. She took a long, thirsty drink, her thoughts tumbling with confusion and arousal.

This was an adventure.

Sputtering and coughing, she lowered the bottle.

"Are you all right?" A frown tugged his forehead low, even as his mouth twitched with the barest hint of a grin.

She waved him away, cleared her throat and took another tiny sip. At least he'd freed her hand. Maybe now she could put two coherent thoughts together. "Okay. First things first."

"Let me guess. Slot machines? I bet everyone tries those first." His grin was nothing short of wicked.

She groaned her frustration. "This marriage, you fool. We need to find out how to undo it."

"Now, Marley, that was a little insensitive." He looked, once again, on the brink of laughter at her expense.

"*Please.* Can we stop this? This teasing and flirting and whatever you're trying to do...I'm not up for it. My God. I got married *drunk*, for heaven's sake, and I can't bear it and I just need to get it undone *now*." Her voice ended on a wobble, despite her best efforts.

But she saw his smile finally slip, and then he sighed. A little defeatedly, she thought. Guiltily?

"All right, listen, Marley. There's really no need—"

The muffled jingle of a cell phone interrupted him and he grimaced. "Damn. Let me get rid of whoever—" He picked up the phone and muttered a quick hello.

Hearing the growly jabber of what was unquestionably her father's voice, Marley could hardly contain her frustration. His *timing*, for heaven's sake.

Taking a deep breath, she focused on calming herself. This was not a situation to approach with a short fuse and a brain clouded with emotion. Seeking a calming distraction, she turned her attention elsewhere. Focused. The lobby, after all, was stunning. And admiring the view certainly beat listening in on a conversation between her father and his number-one peon. She carefully got to her feet and went to inspect a statue.

Watching her, Josh noted with relief that her color seemed a little better. That was good. Maybe she wouldn't throw up again after he told her everything. Promises be damned. He couldn't lie to her. Reluctantly, he forced his attention back to Charles, who seemed more feverishly tyrannical than usual.

"…and with her acting the way she's acting, I just can't risk that, damn it."

Josh frowned. "What? What's going on?"

Charles cursed again. "Get your eyes off the damn showgirls and listen up. I've heard rumors, okay? *Bad* rumors. You've got to keep Marley out there with you for as long as possible."

"What kind of rumors? Is she in trouble?"

"Hell, yeah, she's in trouble. You already knew that. That's why you flew out there in the first place. So you could keep an eye out for her. But things have gotten worse. If what I'm hearing is true, she could be in real danger."

"Danger, how?" Stunned and sobered, Josh glanced at Marley and then turned aside. "What the hell's going on?"

Charles grunted. "I'm hearing rumors of Mafia involvement. No details yet. I'm still checking through police records, and I have Pattie working on the Internet researching for me. I didn't really trust anyone else to help with this."

"Yeah, I know." Josh sighed in frustration, his gaze drawn inevitably to Marley again. She looked impatient. He lowered his voice and spoke quickly. "So, bottom line?"

"Bottom line, keep Marley in Vegas with you."

"Okay. But Charles, I'm going to have to tell her now."

"Hell, are you nuts? Just what do you think she'll do, first thing, when you tell her she's being framed for embezzlement?"

"In her current mood?" Josh closed his eyes briefly. "Hightail it back to Richmond and play Amazon woman. Damn it."

"Bingo. If the Mafia's involved, the stakes get higher. She's liable to get hurt, or worse, if she comes back here and starts asking pointed questions. No, she's safer right where she is, half a country away from Richmond. In a crowded tourist town like Vegas, it's easy for her to be anonymous. Keep her there. I don't care how you do it, how much it costs, anything. Just don't tell her what's going on and stay with her until I give you the clear. Got it?"

"These rumors... You believe what you're hearing? This isn't just playing it safe?"

Charles sighed. "Yeah, I think there's something to 'em. Just a gut feeling. I don't want Marley anywhere near here."

"Damn."

Marley was glaring at him now. But what else was new? Josh mused with vicious humor. At this rate, he might as well get used to her hating him. "Okay, I'll do it. But there's going to be hell to pay later."

"Tell me about it."

Josh hung up and pocketed the phone while Marley reseated herself. She crossed her legs impatiently. "So, my charming ex-to-be, now that you're done chatting, let's get started. Do you suppose these wedding chapels offer quickie divorces, too?"

He forced a casual tone. "Why, Marley. I never took you for such a cynic."

"Given the past few days, I think I have reason to be a little cynical, don't you?"

He conceded that with a reluctant bob of his head, his thoughts racing. "Still, there's no need to ditch your vacation entirely, right?" He spoke musingly. "Are you really so anxious to get rid of me that you'd spoil the rest of the week for yourself? We are in Las

Vegas, after all. Sin City. The Entertainment Capitol of the World. Seems a shame to waste the opportunity. What could it hurt to have a little fun since we're already here? Fun first, business later..."

"A little *fun?*" She spoke with a sarcastic lilt.

"Now, I didn't mean it that way." He grinned at the temper he saw in her eyes. He'd take it over desperation any day. "Unless, of course, you wanted a real honeymoon before the divorce. I'm more than willing. And, to be technically correct, I *did* buy the pleasure of your company for twenty-four hours."

"*What?*"

"You know, the auction?"

The outrage in her expression made him want to laugh, but he resisted. "Calm down. I mean, starting this morning. I didn't pay for any of last night."

Her wordless growl implied any number of obscene threats.

"Hey, I did let you sleep in, so we're getting a late start. But actually—" he overrode her indignant protests "—I was referring to the sights and entertainment. I've never been to Las Vegas before. I think it would be fun to experience it for the first time with you. What do you say we spend the next twenty-four hours just...doing Vegas?"

Marley stared speechlessly at him. He supposed, given what she knew and what she didn't know, he could hardly blame her. After all, he was suggesting that they go sight-seeing before seeing to the minor detail of nullifying a marriage.

She opened her mouth, no doubt to loose a whole assortment of insults upon his deserving head, but he cut her short.

"Aaah." He gave her a teasing look full of mock wisdom. "I see her again."

It was a soft challenge.

Marley's temper rose to it. "What? *What?*"

Completely overwhelmed by the wacko across from her and her crazy situation as a whole, she searched blindly behind and around her. She found nothing of note. "What are you talking about?"

"You." At her even more baffled shake of the head, he grinned widely. "The *other* you. Rational Marley is back in control again, ready to bulldoze over any impulse and squash every temptation."

She paused, stifling with effort her instinctive protest, as doubts wormed their way into her thoughts. He was right. How could she deny what was so obviously the truth? She'd been ready to blackmail, cajole or bully him to the nearest chapel and/or county clerk's office to regain her single status. It was, after all, the only rational thing to do. Rational…

"Is that how you see me?" Marley heard the question as if from a distance, then realized it had emerged from her own lips.

She watched him consider his reply.

Groaning as the silence lengthened, she tipped her head back and gazed at the chandelier above. Its crystals sparkled, reflecting tiny rainbows of light. She remembered her own, utterly pathetic excitement over taking an unplanned vacation to Las Vegas. Though it ranked as an unusual experience for her, normal people took spontaneous vacations all the time.

Now here she was, faced with a real adventure, and all she could think to do was collapse and return to her old ways. Even forfeiting her own less-than-adventurous vacation. She was rational, boring, serious, repressed— "Of course that's how you see me. Why wouldn't you? It's exactly the way I am."

"Are you?"

Not raising her head, she shrugged slightly. "Most of the time. Yes." Then, reluctantly, she lowered her chin and straightened in her chair. "It's not a crime to be sensible."

"No." He studied her, not unkindly. "But anything can be overdone."

"So, in my case, losing control is considered *moderation?*"

He grinned a little. "I guess you could say that."

"So, let me see." She tapped a finger to her chin, lowering her eyebrows in a mockery of deep thought. "Drinking plus singing plus table dancing, plus a bar brawl multiplied by marriage I can't even remember…equals moderation. Go figure. A girl turns her back on reason, just for an evening, and even the dictionary loses all sense."

"Not buying it, huh?" He grinned. "Okay, then try this—have you considered the possibility that, in controlling everything around you, you're limiting yourself, too? Why would you want to do that to yourself?"

She raised an eyebrow. "That doesn't sound like a proper attitude for an ambitious executive. I thought your type prized control of all kinds."

His smile broadened. "There you go again, insisting on limits. But think about this. To get ahead in life, you have to take risks. Taking risks—even reasonable, calculated ones—means forfeiting some control."

"Oh, Lord." She closed her eyes. "Enough. Somehow I just don't feel capable of abstract philosophy right now."

He laughed. "So let it go for a while. Relax and recover. It's Sunday. What can you accomplish today anyway? I doubt any public offices are open. Attorneys' offices are probably closed, too. So why not play today and be reasonable tomorrow?"

She stared at him without responding.

"Come on, Marley. What could it hurt? Just take

twenty-four hours out of an entire lifetime to play and explore a little. Think about it. A twenty-four-hour adventure."

"Oh, I think last night was plenty adventurous, thanks."

He smiled. "It doesn't count if you're drunk and you can't remember it later. I think you need to bring one hell of a memory back to Richmond with you. I'd even volunteer to be your adventure guide, ready to deliver thrills and excitement at your command." He gave her a rakish grin that charmed and coaxed. "Come on, Marley. What do you say?"

A twenty-four-hour adventure to remember for all time. She blinked, feeling a tug at her heart. She recalled how the woman at the airport ticket desk had looked at her while she was collecting her boarding pass. That briefly wistful look in her eyes. Marley had seen that look in the mirror too many times. She was tired of sitting still while other people lived out their adventures. Las Vegas was supposed to be her very own exciting, once-in-a-lifetime trip.

And what could it hurt, after all? Like Josh said, she couldn't begin divorce proceedings until tomorrow anyway. So why not have her adventure today and her sanity tomorrow? The best of both worlds. She cautiously let a smile ease across her face.

Yes. It was her turn. Her adventure. Granted, she sucked at it so far, if the *past* twenty-four hours were any indication. But she could redeem herself with the next twenty-four. She could become a savvy party woman, instead of a stupid one. She just needed practice.

Then tomorrow she would divorce the man she couldn't remember marrying.

Yeah, there was a plan.

"Okay, you're on. Pleasure today, divorce tomorrow."

"You're serious?"

"I am." She studied his wide eyes, feeling satisfaction take root and spread. She could really learn to get used to this. Yes, from now on, she refused to live down to her peg.

She also refused to be bounced around by someone else's whims. On that thought, she leaned forward in her seat and gave him a shrewd look. "But first we need to settle a few details. You're planning on being my adventure guide, right?"

"Right." He looked nonplussed, but his eyes were intent.

"Sounds good to me. Assuming you're qualified. Are you? You've looked pretty much as stuffy and reasonable as me until lately. How do I know you're not going to lead me on some lame adventure that won't fulfill my wildest dreams?"

He raised his eyebrows.

She smiled patiently. "Well?"

"What do you want, a résumé?"

She considered, then nodded. "That would work."

"A résumé. For fun." He studied her thoughtfully. "Okay. I backpacked from coast to coast over spring break one year."

She raised her eyebrows, nodding approval. "That's a good one. Still...I *have* danced on tables." She smiled with mock apology. "Plus, there's the husband I can't remember marrying. Can you top those?"

He gave her a sarcastic look. "You want fun adventures or just plain trouble?"

She glared, then relented. "Point taken." Grudgingly.

He smiled slightly at her tone, then sat forward. "Marley. I'd love nothing better than to give you a thrilling twenty-four hours. Not just pleasant. Not just smiles and postcards home. I want to make you laugh, maybe scream a time or two, and definitely remember this day for the rest of your life."

She held her breath. Oh, yeah. He was right on. He knew and understood exactly what she'd wanted when she started out on this trip. A liberating, heart-racing adventure. In Sin City.

"Is that enough for you?"

She cleared her throat, tried to speak normally around all the hopes that threatened to steal her voice. "Your résumé lacks specifics…but I like the sentiment. You can deliver this?"

He smiled a familiar smile. *I've never had cause to call a woman frigid.* "What do you think?"

She smiled back, excitement pumping through her veins. Plus lots of nervousness. The good kind. "I think you have a deal."

JOSH WAS FEELING a bit light-headed himself. He couldn't believe he'd talked her into a day's reprieve. His whole argument was so outrageous that Marley, in her normal frame of mind, would have told him, quite calmly, to take a flying leap.

But he wouldn't question good fortune. Hell, every day he could beg, steal or borrow would work to their advantage.

What he needed to do now, while they ate lunch—basically refueling before commencing to adventure—was think up some appropriate itinerary for wild and crazy fun that didn't involve lawbreaking, kinky debauchery or serious injury. True, he needed to kill time so Charles could clean up the mess in Richmond, but he also knew he'd better fill that time wisely and creatively—or risk Marley calling his bluff.

They ordered a simple lunch, and Marley settled into it, relaxed and yet not. She'd decided to set aside last night's disaster, just for the day, but it still preyed on the outer edges of her mind. Despite it, despite everything, she was determined to just this once...let life happen. And it was a strange sensation, this going with the flow stuff. She didn't have anywhere she needed to be, no deadlines to make or projects to finish. Not even plants to water. Today was for fun.

She slowed for a moment, fork raised, as she pondered.

"Something wrong?"

She glanced up, startled. "Not really. Just—"

He grinned, slowly. "Finding it hard to adjust?"

She narrowed her eyes.

"Please. You're like an open book with this whole thing, Marley. When's the last time you took time off work to play?"

She shrugged. "It's been a while."

"Longer than that." He eyed her dubiously. "I bet you don't even know how to play anymore."

Her gaze flickered. He was right. She didn't really know what to do with free time. This whole schedule-free mind-set was disorienting. Obviously she needed a change.

She raised her chin. "That's why I have you, remember? I thought you were going to be my private little adventure guide."

He saluted her with his water goblet. "I remember."

"So what's first, guide?"

"First we get the lay of the land." He grinned. "So to speak."

So to speak. She glanced away, trying to erase all mental tauntings of lays of the land, and whether *she'd* been one last night. Surely he didn't expect a repeat performance. She gazed at him suspiciously. No. He wouldn't.

"We'll do The Strip first."

She choked and averted her gaze. *Must* everything sound like an innuendo? Probably. At least
until she remembered the details from last night.
Memories couldn't be forced into the open, so she'd
let them go for a while, but first— "Where are you
staying tonight?"

He gave her an innocent look. "With my bride?"

"Dream."

"Just a joke, Marley. I took a room here at the hotel.
We're covered. Now eat so we can go play."

While she ate, absently contemplating possibilities and a whole lot of thoughts she'd already forbid-
den herself, she saw the skinny guy in the suit. The
one she'd baffled with her "trick question" earlier.
He was two tables over and seemed to be watching
them. Once she made eye contact, he hurriedly returned his attention to his own meal.

Fighting a rush of color and a grin, she supposed
she couldn't blame him for his curiosity. It probably
wasn't every day that a strange woman stopped to
ask him if they'd married the night before.

After lunch, Josh and Marley left the hotel and
strolled down Las Vegas Boulevard, more popularly
known as The Strip. Listening to Josh's rich voice
reading the back of a brochure telling the history and
high points of the city, Marley gawked like the worst
kind of tourist. She didn't care. This was fun.

She gazed, wide-eyed, at Paris Las Vegas's small-
scale Eiffel Tower, and the mock skyline of New York,
New York. The sheer size of the casino hotels and
their stories-high neon signs illustrated the one-up-
manship that had characterized the area from its
first, scandal-ridden inception.

It had been a race for the biggest, the most luxurious, the most outrageous, the most commercial. It
was wholeheartedly tasteless and she *loved* it. Something inside of her, some silly child hidden behind

conservative clothing and a pragmatic mind-set, positively thrilled at the lovely excess as though it were native to some exotic civilization.

After only a few blocks of walking, however, the pumps that were so practical at the office began to chafe in the Nevada heat. It might be mid-September already, but the desert sun was still pushing the thermometer into the nineties. Her discomfort increased. When her winces and odd pacing grew obvious, Josh glanced down at her in question.

"Problem?"

"Yes. My feet are killing me and this sweater is rubbing me raw." She grimaced. "Let's stop in one of those shops ahead."

"Sounds good. I could use some shorts, myself."

"So I heard."

Sweeping her ahead of him with a flourish, he guided her through an elaborate shopping mall, complete with a false sky overhead and an animated statue show. Marley blindly followed in Josh's wake until he led her into a clothing shop.

Then she leveled her gaze on the odd spectacle of Josh Walker poking through racks of shirts, shorts and girlier things. Smiling slightly, she glanced at a price tag and reality smacked her right across the dwindling bank account. She backed toward the entrance. "Oh, no. Let's go someplace else—"

"Don't worry about it, Marley. I can pick up the tab."

"I'm not letting you buy me clothes."

He rolled his eyes. "Lighten up, Marley. A new outfit isn't going to break me."

"You're *not* buying me clothes."

He sighed. "Okay, look at it this way. If you were drunk last night and found yourself in a rotten fix this morning because of it, *somebody* must have steered you into trouble." He grinned. "Well, at least some of it. You did okay on your own for a while there, too."

She gave him a look.

"Seriously, Marley. You seem to hold me at least partially responsible for the mess you're in. Right?" He grinned provokingly. "So why don't you make me pay for it?"

Yesterday's Marley would have said *no thank you.* Today's Marley gave him a bold, assessing look. "Excellent point."

Laughing, he tugged her over to another rack and reached out a hand to caress the chiffonlike fabric of a halter top. An intrigued smile crossed his face as he glanced back and forth between her and the garment. Marley rolled her eyes and felt heat climbing her neck. He was obviously imagining her in the skimpy little top, which she wouldn't be caught dead wearing.

Usually.

Hesitantly, she touched the material. The breezy fabric felt cool and light against her skin, and it was hard to resist the warm teal and bronze hues woven through it. Without looking at him, she snatched the halter off the rack, checked the size, and turned. Josh stood there with a pair of women's jean shorts and a challenging grin. Pausing only briefly to check the size—which, of *course,* he'd guessed correctly—she accepted the shorts, as well, and marched into the dressing room.

After kicking off her shoes and pulling off her sweater and skirt, she stepped into the shorts and tugged them into place. Very short and very low waisted. She swallowed, then persevered. She worked the halter into place, tied the filmy straps behind her neck, then turned to survey the effect in the mirror.

Opaque in front, thank God. She spun around.

But the halter bared nearly all of her back; she couldn't even think of wearing a bra with it. Wow. It was the very last outfit she would have picked out on her own. But she had to admit it looked good on her. She could almost *feel* attitude seeping into her blood. Lovely.

What would Josh say? Glancing up, she met her own eyes in the mirror, surprised to see the devilish gleam in them. Hmm. So maybe he'd been right about a little adventure being good for the soul. She had, after all, suspected. It was why she'd traded in her Denver trip for Las Vegas.

Smoothing the flutter of chiffon over her midriff, she gathered her clothes and her courage and exited the dressing room. Before returning to where she'd left Josh, she paused to try on some strappy bronze sandals that caught her eye. They fit like a dream. And she'd never worn bronze shoes before.

Smiling, she slipped the other sandal on, too, raised her chin and sauntered off to find Josh. He'd obviously done some trying on of his own and now wore a new pair of khaki shorts and a casual shirt and was busy trying on sunglasses.

"You like?"

He glanced back at her in surprise, tags swinging from his sunglasses, then he tugged the shades off and stared. After a long moment, he just shook his head and continued to skim a gaze up and down her body. "Wow. You could do some damage in that."

Given the avid look in his eyes, she'd take that as a yes. *She* could do some damage. Her. Marley Brentwood. Excellent. Exactly what she'd been seeking from an adventure—and a woman did need to dress the part.

Eyes narrowing, Josh swept an upraised finger in a rough little circular motion. Cautiously, she obeyed, spinning so he could see the back of her outfit. What there was of it. She stood there, heart pounding, as he drew closer. He'd be shocked.

Good. That would make two of them.

He wasn't saying anything. Why? Was he thinking about last night? What did he remember that she couldn't? Oh, God, had it been good? She hoped it had been good. But if it had, and she'd missed it, was that good? Why couldn't she remember?

God knows she was remembering everything else. The moments of humiliation were gradually becoming crystal clear—and they were right about her singing abilities, or complete lack thereof—but what about the other moments? The ones that were tickling all over her libido? She'd tried like hell to recall them, but *oh*, no. *Those* memories had to remain a mystery.

"Wow," Josh murmured now, a little dazedly. "I swear to God I never thought I'd see this. Marley Brentwood, you look bold and sexy as hell. Ready to take on the world. It's incredible." He shook his head. "You know, this other side of you—last night and today—she's a force to contend with."

"Last night was someone I don't even know."

"Oh, I've met her."

Marley groaned. "I know. The singing, the dancing..."

"The savvy businesswoman."

She paused and looked up at him. "Sarcasm, right?"

"Nope. I've never had a problem with your business nerve. You have courage, you're smart as hell and some of your ideas are really innovative. Given the proper training and a decent chance, I think you could even run the company if you wanted to. You've worked there how long now? I remember your dad saying you worked part-time and summers during high school and college. And full-time after that. Hell, I bet nobody short of your father has as much hands-on experience with the company as you do."

"You're serious." She stared at him, disarmed.

He shrugged. "It's the way I see it."

"Yeah, well, my father would never see it that way." Cynicism dampened her wonder.

"If you want a man to look at you differently, you have to wake him up a little. That includes your father."

And Josh? She studied him. He was looking at her differently. There was an earthier, intimate cast to his eyes. And then it hit her. He was looking at her as if she was a woman. An approachable one—a viable possibility.

Time to kill *that* possibility in its tracks. "I'm not trying to wake anyone up. I'm doing this for me. And when I go looking for another job, I won't be under any man's thumb."

He smiled approvingly. "Good. It's about time. Shall we?" He reached for the tags she'd taken from her clothing choices.

She felt a lingering, instinctive resistance to the idea of letting him pay, but she shook it off. Meek Marley would pay like a good girl. She wasn't meek Marley right now. With a flourish, she handed him the tags and he reached for his wallet. A salesclerk offered Marley a shopping bag for her old clothes.

While she waited for Josh to pay, Marley casually glanced out the storefront window and happened to see the skinny suit guy from the hotel. With his nonexistent chin, discreetly pinched nose and puffy upper lip, he had a face like a rabbit's, and he was staring directly at her. But as soon as their eyes met, the guy ducked behind his newspaper and disappeared into a neighboring coffee shop.

Marley blinked. Okay, this was getting a little

weird. She supposed he could still be running into them by accident, but—

"Ready?" A voice asked from behind.

"Hmm? Oh, sure. Whenever you are."

"Great." Josh plucked the shopping bag out of her hand and gestured her onward. "Come on, wife." When she winced, he chuckled. "Can't beat it today, so might as well have fun with it right? Hell, look at me. Carrying shopping bags like any other whipped male in the place. I'm in character."

"You're impossible." But she was grinning despite herself. Forget rabbit face; she had an *adventure* to pursue. "Now drop the domesticated act and play fun guide. That means you lead."

He gave a funny half bow and a devilish grin. "Then let the adventure begin."

6

"YOU WANT TO GO SKATING?"

Josh gave her an affronted look. "*In-line* skating. It's *fun*. And I bet *you've* never done it before. Have you?"

Marley blinked. "Well…no. But it doesn't sound like the thrill-seeker fun you've been promising me. And it's *not* what I expected in Las Vegas, of all places."

"You sound like an adrenaline junkie in the making, Marley. Did last night give you a taste for it?" Laughing, he dodged a halfhearted shove from Marley, then snagged her other foot to work a skate on it. For rented skates, they were in decent shape. He hoped his skills were up to keeping them that way.

"Adrenaline junkie." She snorted.

"I calls 'em like I sees 'em."

"Get a life."

He grinned. While he laced up her skate for her, he allowed his gaze to roam a little northward. For such a sensible woman, she had one helluva set of legs. "Do you work out?"

She glanced up, startled. "I do laps at the pool. Some Pilates. Why?"

He smiled down at her. "Nice gams, babe."

She choked. "Thanks. I think."

Once he'd laced up her other skate as well as his own, he stood up from the park bench, prayed for balance and offered her a hand. "Ready?"

She smiled sweetly. "Ready." She took his hand, launched past him and skated off like a pro. Spinning gracefully to skate backward a few feet, she gave him an innocent look. "Did I mention I took ice-skating and figure skating as a kid?"

He groaned and followed with less grace and more determination. "No."

"Four years' worth."

"But never in-line roller-skating."

She gave him a pitying look before skating past.

So, as an adventure guide he sucked so far. How was he to know she skated like a freaking champion? He groused silently, while admiring those legs in graceful action. She'd worn those short shorts at his provocation.

Left to her own devices, he knew, she'd have picked out walking shorts—a longer and baggier version of the skintight little denim scraps she wore now. He'd also happily take credit for the filmy little halter top that flattered an excellent set of breasts and allowed peeks of a flat tummy. And as for the back view...damn.

She glanced up at him, a superior smile on her face. Okay, so he sucked at skating, too. Surely she'd give him credit for braving it for her sake. His gaze sharpened. "Marley, look out."

"What?"

"The pavement—"

She inhaled sharply, then stumbled over an inches-wide crack in the sidewalk. Grabbing her in a clumsy attempt to break her fall, Josh sent them both careening into the wall of a building, with his back taking the brunt of it. At least they were clear of traffic. As other pedestrians and a skateboarder breezed by, he kept hold of her arm. "Sorry. You okay?"

"My fault. But I'm okay. You?"

"Better now." Fully recovered and relieved that she hadn't hurt herself, he shifted to let part of his weight rest against her sexy, scantily clad self. Damn, but he liked that halter on her. Lots of skin. And the shorts—

Catching him in mid-ogle, she flushed and scowled.

He pursed his lips, trying not to smile.

"*My*, but this has been entertaining."

"Sorta depends on your perspective, I guess."

She shoved away from the wall. "Well, you know what you can do with your perspective."

He caught her hand. "Something obscene, I'd imagine."

"And you'd be right. Now let go. If this is your lame idea of an adventure, then at least let me enjoy it."

She checked for traffic and obstacles, then skated back onto the walkway.

He chased after her, ready to give her some of her own back, when he saw him again. The guy from the hotel. Here. Josh had seen the guy shadowing Marley all morning in the hotel, and he'd been at the lounge last night, kind of skulking in the shadows. Not good. The guy wasn't here for a vacation; he couldn't look more out of place if he tried. Skinny, frowning as if he really should be at a funeral and wearing a suit coat. In this heat, and given Josh's own suspicions, the guy could even be concealing a weapon under that jacket.

Definitely up to something. If Josh had been alone, he would have just confronted the guy. As it was—

"Hey, Marley." He caught up with her and snagged her arm until she slowed. She looked down at him, a little disgruntled.

"What? Was I going too fast for you? Some adventure guide."

"Damn. A complete junkie." Despite the seriousness of their situation, he couldn't prevent a grin. "Look. Since this is no big deal for you, I have a better plan. What do you say to thrills by day and traditional Vegas by night?"

She raised an eyebrow. "I'd say it depends on your definition of thrills."

"So suspicious."

She shrugged. "I've been too gullible lately. Cynicism's good for the sanity."

"Ouch." He shook his head. "Now I know I'm on the right track. Let's lose the skates and go for thrills. I think you'll approve. Hey, you're not *prone* to vomiting, are you?"

She gave him a condescending glance. "Trick question?"

He took that for a no. "You'll see."

She rolled her eyes, but looked intrigued nonetheless.

AN HOUR LATER, they emerged from the Stratosphere Hotel, breathless and laughing. Marley admitted silently that she'd had doubts when Josh first pulled out the skates, but he'd redeemed himself with the thrill rides.

"A most excellent adventure, Joshua T. Walker."

"You liked?" He grinned at her.

"Oh, yes. I loved it, in fact. Imagine a roller coaster on top of a tower on top of a hotel. And then the Big Shot. Wow."

He laughed. "Good. I got your attention."

"You did at that. So what's on the agenda now, oh Super Adventure Stud."

"Hey, that's good. Super Adventure Stud. Beats—what was it you called me earlier? Peon? Asshole?"

She blinked innocently. "Oh, I think there was an

assortment. Peon certainly. In fact, it still springs to mind."

Sort of like when she saw another of her father's peons skulking around. The skinny suit guy from the hotel. This guy just *had* to be someone her father had hired to follow her. What other explanation could there be? She'd eat her shoes if the guy turned out to be a stalker with romance or obsession on the brain. The guy just seemed too impersonal about his task to fit that kind of scenario.

He looked distinctly uncomfortable, too. A jacket in this heat? He'd probably croak from heat exhaustion and solve all her problems. Wouldn't that be nice. She resisted the urge to glare openly at the guy. Her beef and revenge were with her father, not this incompetent, rabbit-faced creature.

Still…she silently contemplated. Perhaps the guy could be of some use. If he was reporting back to her father, wouldn't it be entertaining to give him something juicy to report? A girl should really take advantage of those opportunities that presented themselves Not a bad plan at all.

She glanced up, saw the skinny suit guy had moved closer for a better view, and she rode a thrill of daring. Wrapping one bold arm around Josh's neck, she pulled him down for a tongue-thrusting kiss. Ignoring his *mmmph* of surprise, she pressed against him and invested every bit of that outrageous energy in her kiss. And tried desperately to ignore how good he tasted. How good he felt, in fact. Deliberately, feeling as brazen as she'd ever been, she raised her knee high against his thigh, curled her leg around his hips and pulled him yet closer.

There, rabbit face. Nibble on that for a while.

Better yet, why don't you phone home to Daddy Brentwood and tell him all about it. That would teach her father to have her followed. Completely juvenile on her part, but, oh, what a rush.

In so many ways.

When Josh pulled back from the kiss, she had to resist the urge to follow and reclaim that mouth of his. Wow. He was just...yum. Still smiling, over her own nerve and the sensual experience itself, she glanced up into Josh's eyes, and his bafflement finally registered. She let her leg slide off his and felt her cheeks heat up. Of course he was baffled. She'd gone from assorted insults to mauling the poor guy on the street.

"Um...that was a thank-you. For the rides. Thank you." She gave him a firm smile, hoping for the best. Wasn't her gender supposed to baffle his anyway?

"Oh. You're welcome?" He sounded hoarse. Cleared his throat. "You liked the Big Shot, I take it?"

She swung around to keep from facing him and started walking. "It was great. I loved the roller coaster, too. I can't believe they put that thing all the way up there. Amazing."

Josh glanced upward at the tower. "Yeah. Pretty tame as far as roller coasters go, but I guess that's not the point. It's a long way down."

She laughed and nervously pattered on, ignoring her racing heart, Josh's questioning looks and her rabbit-faced spy. Josh was right. She was getting a taste for outrageous adventure. "A looooong way down. Wow, it was fun, though. But you say this was tame? For a roller coaster? I mean, it wasn't as thrilling as the Big Shot. That whole *way* up and *way* down motion left my stomach somewhere in between, but...the roller coaster was tame?" Heart racing, she stopped talking only long enough to demand that he continue talking.

He shrugged. "It was kind of slow and predictable, but I bet it's hard to anchor a roller coaster on top of a building."

"Huh. Well, that makes sense, I guess. Not that I have much experience. This was my first rollercoaster ride." She interrupted herself to veer onto yet another tangent that would lead to yet more distracting talk. "So tell me, then, what's the wildest ride you've ever been on?"

He gave her a teasing smile. "Besides you kissing me just now? Because I gotta tell you that was a really, really wild ride. Nothing predictable about it."

She flushed and stumbled—she'd totally miscalculated.

He grabbed her arm to steady her, then gave her a shrewd look. "Okay, talk. You're up to something. Was that kiss just a Marley adventure? A thank-you? Or more?"

She shrugged. "Does it matter so much?" She smiled and changed tactics. Maybe she could brazen through a fluff-brained explanation. "It *was* an excellent adventure, though. You kiss very well, even with your jaw hanging open." She grinned.

Despite the impact on her nerves and her composure, it *had* actually been pretty amazing. Taking him by surprise like that. She didn't often get that feeling—that she'd acted contrary to other people's expectations. Quite the reverse, in fact. People just expected and she always delivered.

Maybe that would have to change, too. Maybe she didn't regret kissing Josh—for any reason or for anything that she'd felt as a result. She'd loved the daylights out of it, so she refused to rationalize it away or apologize for it.

This could work.

Josh looked thoughtful. "Kissing me is an adventure, huh? Okay. I can deal with that." Amusement flickered in his eyes. "And, should you feel this same urge again, well, go ahead and indulge yourself. I am your adventure guide, after all."

"Don't push it, buddy."

"Er, isn't that *peon?* No, wait. It's *Super Adventure Stud.* I liked that one better."

"Oh, I don't know. Peon's fitting pretty well again."

When he made a lunge for her and she squealingly dodged it, she glanced up and noticed that rabbit face was gone.

Good. He was probably burning up some evil cellphone minutes reporting back to her father. Hmm. She kind of hoped he'd hang around a little more. This could be fun.

AFTER A HIKE BACK UP The Strip, they stopped in again at the Forum shopping center at Caesars for a cool drink and some people watching. Josh watched this new and different Marley. Her face was flushed, a little warm from the day's heat, but radiant with it, too. He smiled when he saw her grin at a pampered pooch strolling by on the end of a rhinestone-studded leash.

"I always wanted a dog, but that seems a little cruel. Even a dog should be allowed dignity." Her smile grew incredulous. "Oh, good grief. The poor thing's toenails are hot pink."

He laughed, still watching her. "Animals don't care as long as they're loved and fed. And this one looks pretty pampered."

"You sound like you'd know. Do you have a pet?"

"Yeah. A bird."

"A bird?" She swung her gaze back to him.

"A blue-and-gold macaw. His name is Lance."

"Lance?" Her lips curved.

Josh draped an arm over the back of their bench, dangling his fingers over her bare shoulder. "I'm not responsible. He named himself."

She started laughing.

"I'm not kidding. That's the only name he answers to."

"Answers? He *talks*." Her voice lowered in amused intrigue. "What does he say?"

Glancing away, Josh mumbled something incoherent. He'd asked for this.

"What?"

Josh sighed, embarrassed. "He likes to repeat stuff he hears on TV."

"Really?"

"Yes, really."

"Like what?" She sounded fascinated. "Commercials?"

"He likes this soap opera." At her raised eyebrows, he rushed to explain and perhaps retain at least the shreds of his masculine dignity. "It's a long story, but let's just say, through trial and error, I finally got the bird to talk. He likes TV—it calms his shrieking fits—and he got hooked on this one soap opera thanks to my housekeeper. She likes to listen to it while she works. That's where he got his first words. Even his name."

She was quiet a moment, then burst into laughter. "Lance? Like Lance Deveaux?"

He raised an eyebrow at her. "So you watch *Worlds of Passion*, too?"

Her eyes widened comically before she glanced away and recrossed her legs.

He laughed, letting his gaze linger for a moment on smooth calves and thighs. "Well, well, well."

"Oh, shut up. I'm entitled to a little escapism, too."

"That didn't sound like casual escapism. I bet you watch it all the time." He narrowed his eyes and grinned. "You *tape* it."

She lifted her chin. "And you don't?"

"I only tape it to keep Lance happy and out of trouble." Even he could hear the defensiveness in his voice.

She started laughing again. "You tape the soap opera every day so your bird can watch it." She looked up at him, her eyes warm and dewy with laughter.

Without even meaning to, he'd found a way past her caution, her suspicions, even her adventure-seeking bravado, to find the soft woman she hid away inside. She was smiling warmly at him right now. The skating, the roller coaster, even the wild kiss…those had all been adventures for Marley. She'd enjoyed them and his company, but this was more. She was focusing on him now. Finally. Not just fun and him. Or being pissed off or feeling betrayed by him. Or being cautious or suspicious of him. Just seeing him as a person. As a man.

"Josh, you surprise me." Her amber eyes glowed with curiosity and interest. "That is such a silly, sweet thing to do. You tape shows for your bird. Soap operas, no less. I bet you even watch them with him."

He grimaced, feeling his neck heat up. "I do not." He paused then gave her a rueful grin. "I don't have to. Lance replays the highlights over breakfast every morning."

She started laughing again.

"So I'm exaggerating a little. He has…favorite phrases." He rubbed a hand over his face. "Please, let me stop. This is humiliating." Despite his embarrassment, Josh couldn't help but smile and chuckle a little in the face of her wholehearted enjoyment. "You'll have to meet him sometime."

"I'd like that. He sounds wonderful." She laughed again, shaking her head. "So where's the bird while you're down here getting into trouble with me?"

Josh sighed, frowning. "Well, right now, my housekeeper's taking care of him, but she's planning to go visit her sister. I'll need to find someone else until—" *Damn.* The last thing he wanted to do was give Marley another excuse to rush a divorce.

Instead, she gave him a crafty, almost evil little grin. "Why don't you have my father watch him?"

"Your father?" He raised an eyebrow. Suddenly, he was assaulted with a vision of her gruff, no-nonsense father staring, astounded, while his bird shrieked amorous nonsense for Charles's dubious pleasure. "What a fantastic idea."

Grinning, he glanced down at her, surprising a wide-eyed look of interest on her face.

"Josh, if I don't watch myself, I could end up liking you."

"We can't have that happening, now can we?"

"No." But she was grinning. He decided that was a good sign.

"I BOUGHT YOU A LITTLE PRESENT." Josh held out a cheerful little gift bag with iridescent tissue peeking out of the top.

"A present?" She gave him a wary look. He must have slipped into one of the shops while she used the bathroom.

"Not that you'd accept it. Nice girl that you are." He didn't even bother to hide the taunting challenge in his voice or eyes. He just watched her, still holding out the bag to her.

She gave him a narrow-eyed look intended to resemble a glare and compressed her lips to hold back a responding grin. He read her too well, and blast him, *no*, she wouldn't have accepted it from him a week ago. She snatched the bag from his hand with a wordless mutter that made him smile. Curious, she dug through the tissue until she saw something shiny. She reached in.

And pulled out something very tiny. Two somethings. "A *bikini*?" She pulled out a larger, but very sheer, something. A cover-up that didn't live up to its name.

"Yep." He grinned. "More adventure plans. What do you say?"

Refusing to back down from the condescending challenge she saw in his eyes, she raised her chin. "Lead on, tour guide."

"My pleasure." The grin on his face, plus the blatant sweep of his gaze from her head to toe, told her his current pleasure was in imagining her in the teeny scraps of gold lamé. Talk about frivolous. Daring—and something she never would have bought for herself. *So* un-Marley.

She smiled. There was an adjective worth obliterating.

Or completely redefining.

JOSH TOOK HER TO A WATER PARK.

"Well." Marley gazed up at the sign with mingled excitement and caution. Then, snagging her courage and her newfound daring, she smiled. "All kinds of firsts in the last twenty-four hours."

"That's what an adventure's all about, I guess. So you've never done this, either?"

"Nope."

He frowned. "No roller coaster. No water park. Hell, why couldn't Charles have taken you to places like this when you were a kid?"

"He was a busy guy." She shrugged. "I wasn't neglected. We just did other stuff together."

"Like?"

"We read together. And it seems like he's been teaching me about business since I could speak." She smiled nostalgically. "I don't think he really knew how to talk to a kid. Just that he should. And he really tried. I know he did."

Josh nodded, seeming to digest that. "I believe it."

"So who took you to roller coasters and water parks when you were a kid?"

He grinned ruefully. "I took myself."

"You went alone?" She frowned. "Your parents let you?"

"Not exactly. It was mostly just Mom and me when I was growing up." He shrugged a little evasively. "So I was on my own a lot of the time."

She frowned. "Sounds a little lonely."

"Not too bad. I had friends. I lived through it." He gave her a curious look. "I bet it was kind of neat, having a live-in mentor like you did, though."

"It had its moments." She glanced ahead of them, noticing that the admission line had begun to advance. "Dad wasn't perfect, but he did his best, I think. We both did. And I'm not abnormally screwed up." She grinned at him.

"Well—"

"Shut up and take me to the park."

Laughing, he slipped an arm around her and led her to the ticket counter. Once they'd paid—Marley insisted on paying her own way, to Josh's disgruntlement—she took a good look around and faced a new difficulty. A truly unusual difficulty.

"I can't do this." She murmured it to Josh.

"Sure you can. You can swim, right?"

She snorted. "Yes, I can swim. It's not that."

"Then what?"

"This outfit. The *bikini*. There are children around here. *Impressionable* children." She hugged the sheer material of her cover-up closer, as though she could force it to be opaque.

He chuckled. "Oh. You mad temptress-slash-pervert you. Afraid of traumatizing the young?"

"Well, yeah. It's a concern."

He rolled his eyes. "Please, Marley. That suit is just fine for mixed audiences. I promise."

"But—"

"Yeah, it's sexy. The metallic thing will garner attention, but you'll be decently covered."

She frowned uncertainly. He could be right. She usually wore a racing-type tank suit suitable for swimming serious laps—and rarely visited any but her gym pool—so her experience was certainly more limited than his. "You're sure?"

"I'm *sure* I'm sure."

She rolled her eyes at his clowning. "Fine. If I get thrown in jail for indecent exposure, you get to bail me out and break the news to my father." She grinned suddenly.

He groaned. "Don't do it. You would regret it."

"I just figured I didn't have much to lose after last night." She gave him a cheeky grin that was so un-Marley—unlike the *old* Marley, the *facade* Marley—that he just stared.

Half an hour later, Josh emerged from frothing water, sputtering and laughing.

Marley popped up right beside him, choking and coughing. "You didn't tell me they were going to dump us out at the end!"

He snorted with good-natured contempt. "It's a water park. You get wet. What else would they do but dump you off the raft?"

Groaning, Marley dunked him again for good measure. When he swam after her, she took off with steady strokes. Giggling and choking, she managed a squeal of her own before he dunked her.

When they finally climbed out of the water, Marley grabbed a towel for a brisk, laughing scrub. Then she wrapped it around herself and tucked a corner between her breasts sarong-style.

Josh shook the water from his hair as a dog would, spraying water droplets everywhere while she laughed. Then he swiped a towel across his eyes and slung it over his shoulder.

As he did so, he looked up and saw the suited guy again. Only, he wasn't wearing a suit this time. Or pants. Just very long, very baggy elasticized shorts and a shirt. He looked uncomfortable, out of place and wholly suspicious.

Damn, what was Donatelli thinking, hiring this idiot. He's not just a snoop. He's an incompetent *snoop.*

Turning back to Marley, he slipped a protective arm around her waist and sought to remove her from the bastard's sight.

Feeling Josh trying to herd her off to the next ride, she put a staying hand on his shoulder. "Could we take a break? I need to catch my breath after that last one."

"Sure. How about we head over here? See if they have something to eat first."

He sounded distracted and a lot less amused than he had been just moments ago. Glancing past him, she saw rabbit face again. He looked sweaty and uneasy. Good. That would teach him to take orders from some nosy, overprotective Neanderthal of a father. With a tiny little smile, all to herself, she decided to give the guy just one more eyeful. More meat for her father. She couldn't wait to read the final report herself.

Whipping off the towel, she slipped arms and lips around Josh and overbalanced them both into a nearby pool. They went under with a splash, to catcalls and whistles. She held him tightly, lips plastered to his, and gave him all she had.

Josh rose to the occasion. Tightening his arms around her, he slanted his mouth across hers and delved deeply between her lips, to caress and explore. When Marley decided one more moment submerged would mean drowning and death, she felt them both breach the surface. More whistles. More catcalls.

She glanced around. *Okay. Kisses draw attention—*

"Marley." Josh sounded choked.

"Sorry. Not enough warning—?"

His eyes were focused on her chest, still pressed to his.

And minus a bikini top.

HER FACE STILL BURNING, and hysterical laughter only a breakdown away, Marley just kept walking. She purposely ignored the man striding next to her. They'd both changed back into street clothes and were currently hiking back toward the hotel.

"You have to speak sometime."

She kept walking.

"You can't blame me for this, you know. For once, I'm *completely* blameless." He gave a sideways shrug that she more felt than saw. "Okay, so going to the water park was my idea. But the rest of it...pulling me into the pool, your top missing and getting tangled up in their filter system... Us getting thrown out of the park by the family-values police—"

She snorted. "I told you that suit was trouble."

"She speaks! A miracle."

She gave him a look and kept walking. "Just how many blocks are we from the hotel?"

"It's close now. I promise."

She muttered doubtfully.

"Come on, Marl. I know you're not mad. And you can't deny we had fun at the park until you lost the suit."

Her lips twitched. "Gee, there's an interesting qualifier. We had fun until I lost my swimsuit."

"Hell, if you'd lost the suit in private, the fun would be just beginning."

"Oooooh. Super Adventure Stud takes the stage once again. So tell the audience, Stud. Are you all talk or is there action to back it up?"

Still walking, still reeling from her brush with indecent exposure, she had only spoken with absentminded humor born of a need to conceal her nervousness. They had, after all, been flirting most of the afternoon. Harmlessly, cheerfully. This was just more of—

He grabbed her arm, spun her around and planted his lips on hers. It was, actually, the first time he'd initiated a kiss—

Her thoughts melted and her knees bobbled. Slanting his lips across hers, he tugged her closer and held on tight, as though he could impress upon her that this was the real deal. No teasing pretext for benefit of a rabbit-faced snoop. No testing of the waters just to see… No, this was the *real, heart-thumping deal.*

Tangling her fingers in his shirt, she held on, immersed herself completely in that kiss. Wallowing in her curiosity, his boldness, her adventuring spirit. And more. This wasn't just an adventure. She could crawl right inside of him and drown in mindless bliss.

Shaken, Marley pulled free and stumbled backward until he caught her, gently, then released her.

"Wow."

She blinked, studying him. "Wow?"

"*Oh,* wow." He seemed to breathe heavily, too.

"I've never…*wowed* a guy before." She tilted her head, intrigued and even more turned on. "You're not putting me on, are you?"

"Why would I do that?" He gave her a baffled look. She stared back.

With a frustrated snort, he raked a hand through his short, still-damp hair. The action raised sexy spikes over his crown, giving him a dangerous, frustrated look. "Your father again, right? You honestly think I'd go that far? Why?"

"I don't know." She glanced away.

"Hey." He waited until she turned back to him. "Why is it so hard to believe that I want to kiss you? That I find you attractive? *You*—not your father's daughter."

She gazed at him in shock.

"Of course I know that's what you've been thinking. You think no guy can get past your father to see you. It's not true. Give it up, Marley. You're a sexy woman, and I guarantee your father would not approve of what I'm thinking right now." He grinned at her.

She raised an eyebrow, ignoring the heat in her cheeks.

"Why so shy now? Why the blush?" He gave her a curious look. "In the water park, hell, even before that, at the Stratosphere, you're the one who started heating things up between us. You kissed me. If you honestly thought I didn't want you, why would you bother?"

She shrugged casually, remembering rabbit face watching them both times. She swallowed hard at a sudden thought. She wondered how her father would take the news that his daughter had gone topless in public.

Her lips twitched. The picture became clearer. Her father. Baffled. Shocked. Enraged. Embarrassed. Speechless?

She swallowed a chuckle. She'd never have *planned* anything that outrageous, but…

"You gonna share that?" He was giving her a challenging look that made her really want to laugh. He looked almost as harassed as the mental picture of her father.

"Nope. I think it's something I'll keep to myself."

"Have it your way then. Women." With a wry glance and a lopsided grin, he took her arm again. "Come on. Something else we have to see."

"More?" She was surprised, pleasantly so.

"Yep. We've done skates, roller coasters, water parks—not to mention last night's bingeing and depravity—" He chuckled at the look she gave him. "So what's left?"

7

A CIRCUS. NATURALLY. This was Las Vegas. Of course there would be a circus, even an entire hotel devoted to the worship of circus fun.

"This is beyond tacky." Marley gazed around, laughing. "I love it."

Josh frowned with mock concern. "Your standards seem to sink lower the longer I spend in your company. Could I be a bad influence on you?"

"I sure hope so."

He laughed. "Good. Come on."

At his urging, they meandered around to watch jugglers and acrobats and various other performers. Marley was so wide-eyed while watching a high-wire act that Josh winced and raised an eyebrow. "Another first?"

"Stop it. I'm not deprived. I'm enjoying myself."

He gave her a searching look, then, satisfied, smiled at her. "Maybe I'm glad you missed out on all this before. I don't think today would have been nearly as entertaining if it wasn't all new to you. It's fun seeing it all through your eyes."

"I believe you really mean that." She smiled up at him. "Why Josh Walker, you can be a nice guy."

"Hey, don't let it get around, but—" He frowned. "*What?*"

She was glaring over his shoulder. "Enough is enough."

That said, she swung around him and cornered her prey by the cotton-candy machine.

"Okay. You." She latched on to a bony elbow and glared into his squinchy face. "What is your problem? It was funny at first, but now you're going to stop following me or I'm going to notify the police. I'm sure there's some law you're breaking."

Rabbit face looked down his bony nose at her. "I don't know what you're talking about. I'm just being a tourist like all the others." His cheeks twitched nervously.

"Sure you are. You seem to be having just a dandy time here at the circus." Her voice lilted with sarcasm. His pruny expression and pursed lips spoke of nothing more than distaste. No way was he here for pleasure. And he was ruining hers.

"You know about him?" Josh stared in surprise.

Her attention snapped abruptly back to Josh. She stared at him, unconsciously relaxing her grip enough for her prey to escape. "*You* know about him?" Her belly tightened with bitter disappointment. "You knew all along that he was following us?"

"Well, he sucks at it. How could I miss it?" Josh stared after the guy, his jaw clenched against his obvious urge to pursue.

She didn't care. *Run, rabbit, run—just leave me the hell alone.* "Oh, Josh. I was really starting to believe in you."

"What are you talking about?"

"All this. Here. Las Vegas. It's all just a pretense. I don't know for sure why you're going through with it." She frowned, studying him fiercely. "For all I know, you've decided to accept that deal with my father after all."

He shook his head, baffled and gesturing impatiently. "God, I thought we were past all that. What does it take to convince you—" He slashed a hand through the air. "Never mind. What's that have to do with the guy who's following us?"

She stared, her anger dissipating. "Following *us?*"

He raised his eyebrows with implied sarcasm. "*Ye-es?*"

"Why would my dad have *you* followed?"

Josh lowered his eyebrows. "He wouldn't. And if he did, he'd sure as hell hire someone more competent than that guy."

She gave him a confused look. "I thought so, too, but—"

"But nothing. He's not working for your dad. I'd stake my reputation on it."

Her frown eased. "Then who, I wonder."

Josh raised an eyebrow. "Maybe a jealous boyfriend you dumped recently? That would be my guess."

Marley scoffed. "Jealous, ha. I doubt me breaking it off with him disturbed a single hair on his head."

Josh smirked. "He is pretty, isn't he?"

Marley rolled her eyes, suppressing a grin. "I'm serious. I don't see him as the jealous type to have me followed. Unless…" She grimaced. "Okay, he might have a lucrative business prospect followed. I suppose that would be me."

Although she'd still reserve judgment on the snoop's income source. Her father had surprised her—and not pleasantly—in the very recent past. Could be her father. Could be Larry. Neither seemed to give a second's thought to her feelings.

Josh studied her then nodded slowly. "Larry's an idiot, you know." His voice lowered. "If he had half a brain in his head, he'd never have let you go."

She glanced away, unsure. Words were so easy. Even Larry knew how to use them when he tried, and God knows, in retrospect, she could see Larry had been less than subtle. He couldn't even pretend passion for her convincingly—yet never once had she seen through his act. "I don't think I was his type. Even if he wanted me to be."

Josh smiled slowly. "Good. *Mine.*"

Her eyes widened, but he was already tugging her onward.

"Let's go check out these fountains I read about."

She went along with him, didn't protest when he slid an arm around her waist, just shifted her arm to give his hand a place to rest. As she did so, a glitter caught her eye. The ring.

Okay, technically, she really was his. For now.

THAT EVENING THEY ATE DINNER at the top of the 'Eiffel Tower,' where Josh affected a mock-French accent as he read her the choices from the menu. His delivery verged on ridiculous.

"Oh, God. Stop—*please.*" Marley, who spoke the language fluently, was laughing so hard tears threatened.

He grinned, completely shameless. "I sound like a cheap Scandinavian whore, don't I?"

She snorted helplessly, laughing harder. The description was so apt.

He just shook his head and chuckled, letting his gaze rest—affectionately, she would swear—on her smiling face. "Damn. It's just amazing."

"What? Your appalling accent? Frankly, I'm not surprised. I've always suspected you had a few flaws."

He grinned. "But they're such attractive flaws." The grin faded to a curious smile. "But that's not what I mean. You. You're amazing. You kept up that composed little front for me for so long. I'd always suspected there was a smart, appealing woman behind the cool smiles and smooth voice. But the sense of humor is a surprise bonus. You're a hell of a lot of fun to play with when you want to be, Marley Brentwood."

She gazed back at him, touched almost to the point of awkwardness. "Yeah? Well, what do you know? Although it is really easy to have fun around you." She smiled crookedly. "You're a bona fide pro at this adventure-guide business. I still can't believe you managed to talk me into this crazy day. And yet here I am. When tomorrow I'll be... Oh, God." She gave him an appalled look. "Last night. Wedding. Tomorrow. Divorce. How could something like that escape my thoughts even for a *second*? I've completely lost my mind."

"Shh. No, you haven't. You're just not dwelling on what can't be changed today. Tomorrow will come soon enough." He paused, then smiled coaxingly. "Tonight we're still on your adventure. Remember?"

"Right. I remember. Okay." She took a deep breath. "Josh?"

He raised an eyebrow.

"For the record...I've enjoyed every minute of today. Except, well—" She paused uncertainly, then raised her chin. "Except nothing. I regret none of it."

"Good. You have nothing to regret." He smiled, but his voice was solemn when he spoke. "And no matter what happened before or what happens tomorrow or later, I want you to know that I loved adventuring with you today. And I hope it won't be the last day we spend together."

Before she could question his solemn words, he smiled and reached across the table to take her hand. "I'm glad you quit your job. I'm glad you broke your engagement. And I'm thrilled as hell you decided to share Las Vegas with me."

She gave him a mischievous grin. "It's still not over yet."

He laughed. "No. It's not even close to over. I still need to show you off." He let his gaze roam low and then, slowly, return to meet hers. "You're way too glamorous to keep to myself tonight."

She gave him a playful look. "Think so?"

"Damn straight. You look utterly dangerous in sequins, lady. You were made for them, with all that fiery hair of yours, reflected back a billion times over."

"No kidding?" She glanced down at the strapless gold-sequined dress she'd impulsively bought for this evening. *Dangerous.* Marley Brentwood. How utterly shocking. Sinking into the notion, she affected a vampy look. "That's me. *Dangerous.* Look out, Las Vegas."

He laughed, then narrowed his eyes in teasing speculation. "You know what? I think you're going to love the casinos."

She raised an eyebrow. "Casinos? Me? I doubt it."

He just smiled, raising his glass in a toast. "We'll see."

Oh, but he was *right,* Marley discovered later that evening. She was appalled at herself, but the excitement level in the room, in herself, in all the lights and rings and flipping of cards, rolling of dice, was irresistible. She gazed around, absorbing the colors and sounds. A half moon of blackjack players lined a nearby table, some serious faced and sweating, some excited and carefree. A magnificent money wheel spun dizzyingly to the delight of a handful of observers. Slot machines, an endless array of them, spun and clanged with endless possibilities.

"Marley?"

"Yeah?" Still, she couldn't keep her gaze in any one place. A quiet craps table nearby erupted with shouts and groans at the roll of a dice.

"Are you ready to try your luck?"

"What? Oh, no." She glanced up at him, distracted

still. "I'd love to watch, though." It wasn't that she was so enthralled with the idea of gambling herself; she just loved the reckless atmosphere. More vicarious living, she supposed, but this time it didn't bother her. This wasn't the kind of risk she was overly tempted to take. The businesswoman in her absolutely rebelled against any but the lightest of gambling. Still, she could get addicted to the sheer energy in the room.

Strong arms slid around her waist and pulled her back against a man's broad warmth. She felt Josh's low chuckle deep in his chest, his breath stirring the hair by her ear. Suddenly, all of her attention was on the man behind her, the feel of a hard chest against the bare skin of her back. She felt less than dressed.

Well, not as undressed as this afternoon at the water park, but…maybe in some indefinable way, she did feel more vulnerable. She and Josh had built something today without her even being aware of it. At some point, they'd crossed over from uneasy alliance to friendship. Probably more.

Whether this was a good thing or not was open for debate.

Still standing behind her, Josh lowered his head to brush his cheek against hers, and she could feel the smile curving his lips. The clean scent of aftershave clouded her mind.

"Marley, Marley, Marley. So controlled and businesslike at the office, but underneath it all, sexy as hell and hungry for adventure. Do you know what that combination does to a guy?"

Her heart pounding, Marley let the bravado carry her a step further. "Why don't you tell me?"

He murmured deeply. "It fascinates him. And challenges him. Marley, all I can think about is hauling you off to bed to see what other surprises you have for me."

Her breath grew shallow. "Other adventures, you mean?"

"You're killing me." He groaned, half laughing, and tightened his arms around her.

The rasp in his voice sent a thrill down her spine and back up again. He really meant every word he said. He wanted her—she really was driving him batty with lust.

What a concept.

And her imagination was supplying vivid detail. What could happen. What she hoped would happen. What she could *make* happen. She caught her breath, shaken by her own nerve.

Severely tempted, she let her eyes drift closed as he nuzzled behind her ear, pressed a kiss to the side of her neck. His fingers, resting just below her breasts, began to lightly knead at tender flesh—making it hard to breathe, let alone think. Could she *possibly*...would she...?

A sudden cheer went up at a nearby table. A man backed into her, jostling her out of a sensual trance set by Josh and her own imagination. Aware suddenly of the noisy crowd, the eyes and laughter, she pulled free of his arms, her thoughts whirling.

She could hardly believe how close she'd let Josh get to her. Only days ago, she'd seen him as just another appendage of her father—someone her father could use to control her.

Now, with just a few words and a provocative touch, Josh had, literally, made everyone and everything around her fade from her consciousness. Including her former fiancé and her most recent decision to leave her father's dominance behind.

Ah, but the charmer was still her father's vice president, still under her father's influence and still ambitious. She wondered how much that ambition had contributed to Josh's sudden desire for her. He'd denied it so far, but what man wouldn't?

Maybe her father had engineered *this* marriage, as well.

Marley whirled to confront Josh. She saw their rabbit-faced snoop disappear behind a row of slot machines, but at the moment she didn't care. It just spurred her onward, gave her more evidence that she didn't like.

But Josh was her focus. *He'd* made it personal.

"Does my father know you're here?"

His eyes flickered in surprise, and she knew the truth.

"*Damn* it. I should have known." She whirled and forged a path through the crowd.

"Wait a minute. Marley." He grabbed her arm and, ignoring her efforts to pull free, he towed her to a little corner table in the adjacent lounge. "Just sit. We'll talk."

Pursing her lips at the command, Marley sat nonetheless and waited to hear what tale the man would spin. It was hard, after all, to walk away and never speak to her *husband* again. She was stuck with him until she got the damn divorce.

Sighing, Josh dropped into a chair next to her. She watched him rake a hand through his short hair. It was an appealing mannerism of his that, unfortunately, had the power to do more than piss her off.

And that self-knowledge only pissed her off more.

"Well? *Talk.*" She gave him a derisive look.

His lips tightened, but he spoke evenly. "I'm not here on your father's orders. He knows I'm here and why I came, but that's as far as it goes. I felt responsible for you."

"Responsible for *me?*" She stared, surprised and annoyed. "I'm an adult and responsible for *myself*, thank you very much."

"Yes, but I was the one who told you—and not

very tactfully at that—about Larry's deal with your father. You were upset, and that was at least partly my fault."

"You were just the messenger. I don't blame you for that." At his skeptical look, she shrugged. "Okay, I was mad at you at first. So sue me. I'm human. It was humiliating."

"And what about now?" He watched her intently.

"Now, I just want to know if I've exchanged one sellout of a fiancé, for a *bought-and-paid-for* husband."

"Nobody buys me. Nobody." She saw instant fury in his eyes, complicated by something more elusive. Memories, perhaps.

"All right. So he didn't buy you. At least not outright."

"Not in any way, shape or form." He leaned forward. "I might also point out that *I'm* the guy who paid a good chunk of money to spend time with *you*."

The auction. Furious all over again, she tried to slide from her chair. "Fine. I'll pay you back." But, hampered by her dress, she couldn't get past a table leg on one side and Josh's big body hovering close on the other. "Now *move*."

He didn't budge. "Damn it. I didn't mean it like that. You just pushed a hot button." He sighed and continued in a more moderate tone. "Honest to God, Marley, I was just trying to look out for you. You were drunk, and I didn't want to think what would happen if you ended up with some strange guy last night."

"I still ended up with *you*." She glared at him.

His lips twisted. "Yeah, but at least *I'm* accountable."

She closed her eyes. Adventure or no, the man had a point. Last night could have ended in worse than mere humiliation. "Yes, you are. And thank you.

For looking out for me." Then she met his eyes. "But you'll still tell me how much money you paid at that auction, and I *will* pay you back."

"Okay. But for right now, could you just hear me out?"

She supposed she owed him that much. "So talk, then."

"It's very simple. What's between you and me has nothing to do with money or ambition. And definitely nothing to do with your father. Hell, the man's been more hurt than help in my dealings with you." He gave her a rueful look.

No denying that. She studied him a moment. "But if my father didn't buy you, why did you marry me last night? We hardly even spoke outside of the office until today."

"What can I say? You're an attractive, desirable woman. Even more so when you let yourself go." His lips curved wryly. "It's enough to make any man lose his head and take a few risks. Especially if he's had a few drinks himself."

"That's it?"

He shrugged. "I could ask you why a rational woman like yourself would marry a man like me. Based on nothing more than a few drinks."

Unable to argue that particular point, she didn't reply.

"So are we okay now?"

"I guess so." She took a deep breath then exhaled slowly on a smile of apology. "Except I don't know a thing about gambling. Can I watch you bet for a while?"

He smiled acceptance. "Sure."

He motioned for her to lead, and they wound their way into the heart of the crowded casino. She observed while Josh played a few hands of blackjack, then followed him over to the craps table. She stood back and watched it, too, and grew increasingly intrigued by the game and the players' excitement. Grinning, Josh tugged her into the play. "Come on. Give it a try."

She couldn't turn down the challenge. Not and still face herself in the mirror the next morning.

Stepping up to the table, she rolled the dice.

When, against the odds, she actually won her throw, she surrendered to sheer jubilation. She did an outrageous little jig that felt blurrily familiar, right there on the casino floor. It didn't even feel un-Marley. It felt wonderful. She looked up into Josh's eyes and saw her own feelings reflected there: excitement, mutual understanding, affection. And an attraction that was increasingly hard to deny.

She'd never admit it aloud, but she suspected that, if it weren't for her father, she'd actually be open to a relationship between Josh and herself. He was fun, witty and intelligent. She genuinely liked him. He also made her libido stand up and take notice more than any man she'd ever dated.

For most of the day, Marley had waffled between wanting to remember and *not* wanting to remember what had happened in her hotel room the night before. She'd needed to remember—even experienced some lurid curiosity about the sexual details—but she'd also feared the humiliation would be the end of her. After all, she'd made love to a man she hardly even knew—didn't even *like* at the time, for heaven's sake—when she was too drunk to even remember the experience.

But now…after this day of thrills, laughter, the occasional scream and some kisses that had rocked her world…she'd grown to like Josh in spite of herself. More than that, she appreciated him, enjoyed him. And she was curious.

No, she was *covetous*.

Good or bad, she wanted those memories back.

And she wanted *Josh*. She shouldn't, but she did.

She wanted to touch him again and let him touch her. Any way and every way. She'd bet he liked to laugh in bed. And tease. And that she could bring herself to tease him right back.

She wanted to remember.

He was big, his body hard. He must be strong. Had he carried her to bed last night? She could still feel his arm against her bare back as she slid between the sheets. It was her one and only memory of them last night, and her heart stumbled over it every time she tried to recapture the experience.

Catching her staring at him, Josh gave her a questioning look. Feeling confused and overstimulated, she gestured meaningfully toward the exit.

Once they'd left the casino and hotel behind them, Josh slid an arm around her bare shoulders. He seemed entranced with the play of streetlights and neon on the sequins of her dress.

"You're staring."

"I can't help it." He smiled, not bothering to conceal his fascination with her body glittering beneath lights.

"Well, you're making me self-conscious. Like I'm going to trip or something." She gave him a flustered look.

He laughed. "Get used to it. I love looking at you."

"There's nothing to get used to. It's all temporary." *Should* be all temporary. *Had* to be all temporary. "Just a little fantasy adventure we'll be ending tomorrow."

Tightening his arm around her, he turned and drew her close. "I don't want it to end. I think today was a hell of a lot more than a little fantasy. There's something real here. Something important."

"But it can't be real." She looked up, resting her

elbows on his chest to reserve a few inches' space between them. "I hardly know you. Sure, we had fun today. But other than your pet bird, the only concrete thing I know about you is what you do for a living." She grimaced. "And who signs your paycheck."

"Your father's company."

"My *father*."

"No. I work for your father's *company*. I don't answer to your father. At least, not for much longer. I've been holding off telling you because the details aren't settled yet, but—" He grimaced then gave her a straight look. "Did your father tell you that I'm buying Brentwood Electronics?"

8

MARLEY FROZE. "You're what?"

"If all goes well, I'll be buying your father's company." Josh studied her face. "We've been negotiating for weeks now."

"But why? My father's never wanted anything but that company. Ever since my mom died, that's where he's lived and breathed. The office. Why would he sell it to you?"

Without even telling me. He'd never even considered...

Josh shrugged. "That's something you'll have to ask him. I just want you to know that your father doesn't own me. I'm here because of you and me. Nobody else. I swear it."

Hesitantly, she nodded. "All right." The company was her father's. She had no claim on it. In fact, she'd rejected it just days ago. Still... She shook it off, seeking distraction. "So tell me more."

"About what?" He frowned.

"About *you*."

Seeming at a loss, he shrugged, and the movement was enough to shift her whole body. He laughed. "I'm bigger than you?"

That sparked a reluctant chuckle. "And I suppose, like all men, you think that's pretty much all a woman needs to know?"

"*Oh*, no. You're not going to trap me with that one."

She laughed.

"Seriously, Marley, there's really not that much to tell."

"Sure there is. Why do you do what you do? What's your family like?" She cocked her head to the side.

"This feels like an interrogation."

She raised an eyebrow. "I feel like you've been picking *my* head apart since you got here. So it's your turn. Why do you work for my father?"

"I respect your father. And I want his company."

"Why?"

"Persistent, aren't you?"

She smiled innocently. "It's one of those qualities you've decided you like about me, remember? The savvy businesswoman? She's terribly persistent. And you should answer the question."

"I respect your father's work ethic and I want what he has. I'm not trying to take it from him, though. I want to buy it."

She gave him a shrewd look. "So why didn't you just make him an offer?" Then, with a rueful smile, she answered her own question. "You wanted an insider's view first. Very smart."

"But once I hired on, I never hid my intentions from your father. I think they amused him. He's toyed with me a little."

"That sounds like him." She nodded. "I really do think he respects and trusts you, but he also likes control."

"As does his daughter. In her own way."

"I suppose so." She shifted his attention. "So tell me about your family."

"There's that persistence again."

She raised an eyebrow, just waiting.

"My father was gone a lot when I was little, and then he died when I was twelve, so my mother raised me. She had to scrape a bit to make ends meet, but we did okay."

She eyed him silently for a moment. "You surprise me."

"Why?"

She lifted a shoulder in a half shrug. "I guess I pictured you with a privileged background. Old money, good schools."

"No money. *Scholarships* to good schools. I worked my ass off to get that education. Maybe that's why I've been so ambitious since then. Put education to good use and turn it into money and influence. Like an investment."

She nodded, intrigued and mentally readjusting. "You know, I remember my father saying he was lucky to get you on board. A few other companies were actually *competing* to get you?"

He shrugged but didn't elaborate.

She nodded thoughtfully and went seeking again. "So what about your mom? Are you close to her?"

He smiled, apparently amused or possibly pleased by her curiosity. "We keep in touch, but no, we're not close. We have…different philosophies on life."

She studied his face. "How so?"

"She likes to marry money. I like to make my own."

"Ouch."

He smiled a little. "That was the shorter, unsympathetic version. She had it pretty rough with my father and she didn't have a lot of earning power after he died." He gazed over her shoulder. "And I think she really cares about the guy she's married to now. The other two…" He shrugged. "Maybe not."

Marley nodded, concerned, and continued quietly. "What happened to your father?"

He inhaled, collecting his thoughts. "You could

say his obsessions caught up with him." Josh nodded at the casino over his shoulder.

"He was a gambler?" That surprised her.

"He preferred the tracks and the stock market, but yeah, a gambler. He liked taking risks. Needed the thrill, I guess. He ended up broke and desperate, died of a heart attack."

She gave him a searching look. "It's pretty amazing, then, that you ended up the way you did. Ambitious. Successful."

"Not really. Some kids take after their parents. Others...vow not to be like them."

She nodded slowly, then frowned.

"What?"

"It just surprises me. You encourage me to take risks, but it was the same risk-taking that brought your father down."

Josh smiled slightly. "Not exactly. My father took risks for the sake of taking risks. To escape a life he hated. I'd like to see you take risks to experience life. See the difference? One's constructive, the other's *de*structive."

She grinned ruefully. "And I know you're a closet philosopher. See how much I'm learning? Tell me more."

He chuckled. "Demanding woman." He shifted her in his arms, linking his hands companionably behind her back. She snuggled closer and he glanced down at her. "Are you cold?"

"A little." The temperature had dropped thirty degrees since noon.

He ducked to share his body heat with her.

"So what's next, Josh?"

"Next after what?" He was obviously still entertained by her questions.

"Once you own my father's company, what will you do next?"

He glanced down in surprise. "Then I run the company."

"Will you like it?"

He shrugged, obviously a little disarmed by the question.

She studied him curiously. "I wonder."

"You wonder what?"

"I just wonder if it will be enough for you." She paused thoughtfully. "If there's anything I've learned about you since you came to Brentwood Electronics, it's that you're enormously ambitious. I don't think you'll just buy my father's company and then stagnate."

"No, probably not."

"You like a challenge."

"True enough."

"So, once you buy my father's company, what challenge will you pursue next? Bigger? Better? More?"

"Probably." But he was frowning.

She continued slowly. "My father seems to look to you as an advisor. He's made that pretty obvious for the past few months. And he's not a man to casually let others have a share in the decision-making."

Josh nodded thoughtfully.

She tilted her head back to meet his eyes. "Have you ever considered going into consulting?"

"No."

She just nodded, aware that she'd started the wheels turning in his head regardless. "Just a thought. Come on. Let's walk." Pulling back, she smiled at him and held out a hand.

"Hold on." He shrugged out of the coat to his tux and draped it over her shoulders. Then, smiling, he grabbed her hand and they strolled some more. Slowing as they neared a small crowd, they stopped to watch a huge man-made volcano spew smoke and natural-gas flames to the appreciation of observers.

Marley grinned. Utterly brazen flamboyance. It was a quality she could really admire—even mildly aspire to, if she let herself.

After the display died down and they resumed their walk, Marley slowed and seemed to gather herself.

"Josh?" She sounded unusually hesitant.

"Hmm?"

"Can I ask you a question?"

He grinned wryly. "I haven't stopped you yet."

Her responding smile was fleeting. She glanced away. "I have to know. Last night. You and me... How were we?"

Damn. He stared. How was he supposed to answer that?

"Well?" It was a challenge born of discomfort. "Was it so bad you don't want to talk about it?"

Coming to a sudden decision, he tugged her into his arms. When she trained her eyes somewhere around collar level, he tipped her chin up and waited for her to meet his gaze.

"You were wonderful last night. So incredibly desirable." He spoke nothing but the truth. Even back in Richmond while ignoring him at the office, she'd always intrigued him. But when he'd seen her last night and still today...her enthusiasm and uninhibited enjoyment... Hell, she'd dazzled him.

Emotion flashed in her eyes before she ducked her head and spoke quietly. "Look, I realize this kind of thing is no big deal for lots of women these days."

"But you're not lots of women."

She looked up. "No, I'm not. I'm not much of a drinker, I don't sleep around— Josh, I just don't *do* this kind of thing with every guy who happens to catch my eye."

"So you're saying I just 'happened to catch your eye' last night?" He smiled, hoping to tease her out of her self-recriminations. "You really are hell on a man's ego."

It had the opposite effect. "How would I know what it was like between us last night? It's all a blur. I can't stand this not knowing."

Seeing real distress in her eyes, he dropped the teasing. "I imagine it's frustrating? Unnerving?" He studied her face, feeling a twinge of guilt. A big one.

"There's an understatement. Have you ever forgotten something as big as a wedding ceremony and—" She broke off. The "and" part seemed to bother her more than the ceremony. Groaning, she fisted her hands in his shirt. "You know what last night was? A *total loss of self-control.*" She enunciated the words precisely, obviously aiming them directly at herself.

He couldn't allow that. "So you cut loose a little. Big deal. Everyone does once in a while."

"Not everyone 'cuts loose' and winds up *married.* Last night was way over the top, no matter how you look at it."

"Not everyone's been saving it up as long as you have. You were overdue for some fun and maybe a huge mistake or two."

"Oh, please." She rolled her eyes.

"Come on, Marley. Hell, look at everything you had to endure this morning. Lost memories, a mysterious ring on your finger, finding me. A lesser woman would have been drooling and rocking herself in the corner."

He smiled fondly, admiringly. "But not you. Not only did you recover from your less-welcome surprises, but you also gave me one hell of an adventure today. Frankly, I think you could handle anything if you put your mind to it."

She stared up at him, a wondering look in her eyes. "You are just full of surprises, aren't you."

"Me?" He blinked. When had they switched gears?

She shrugged, frowning slightly as if searching for the right words. "I guess I've been used to seeing you in the same light as my father. Domineering, a little cold. Single-minded." Her slight smile offered apologies. "But you're not."

She looked confused for a moment, shook her head, then looked intently into his eyes. "You really see *me*, don't you? Not just competent, rational Marley, but the me underneath all that. The one who might enjoy a Las Vegas adventure. Complete with thrill rides, casinos and a walk in the moonlight wearing a sequined nothing of a dress."

Stunned that *now*, of all times, she would choose to realize… It took him a moment to find words. Any kind, even the most shallow ones. He cleared his throat. "Well, I *have* had my eye on you for months now. Makes it hard not to see you."

She moved closer, her eyes and voice so intense. "But, see, that's all part of it. You actually *want* me, too. All of me. Rational, adventurous, bold, shy, all of it. And I can see that every time you look at me now. That's so alien to everything I've ever known from a man."

She believes. Finally. "And this is good. Right?" He didn't bother to mask his desire for her, just let her see it and decide whether she'd accept it or not. He was hoping for—

"Yes." She returned his stare, as though too fascinated to look away. "Very, very good."

Oh, God. He teetered for a moment: temptation versus consequences. He shouldn't. Not now. He wanted to, but he damn well *shouldn't*—

"Josh?"

"Oh, *hell*." Damning her timing and his, he hauled her close and slanted his mouth across hers to delve deeply into the moist warmth. She tasted so sweet, sweeter than any dream he'd ever had of her. And it only drove his desperation deeper, made it that much harder to resist. He knew he should resist. She would hate him if he didn't. As he would hate himself for hurting her.

Because he loved her.

He froze. Where the hell had *that* come from?

But it was true. Stunned, he withdrew and stared into her eyes. *Marley*. There she was. His.

"Josh…?"

A shrill ring cut off whatever either one of them might have said.

"Damn." He could ignore the call, but there was too much at stake back home—too much that affected Marley. Reluctantly, he pulled the cell phone from his pocket and flipped it open to glance at the display. It was her father's home number.

Then he saw a controlled expression wash across Marley's face. The moment was over, apparently. Would she take it all back now?

Grim, he put the phone to his ear. "Yes?"

"Where the hell are you now? There's no answer in your room—" The tinny voice was loud.

"I'm still in Las Vegas, like I told you. Your daughter is here with me." Keeping his voice level, Josh willed the older man to speak more discreetly. "And your timing stinks."

"Let me talk to her."

Josh paused, then held the phone out to Marley.

She stared at it for a moment, her expression carefully blank and her emotions in total upheaval. To go from that kiss and something she might have seen in Josh's eyes to…this? Reluctantly, she accepted the phone and fought for composure.

"Hello?"

"Hi, honey." Her father sounded uncomfortable but concerned. "Are you okay?"

His question caught her off balance. As an adult, she was more used to his businesslike tone, brisk instruction and brief inquiry. Not concern and this vague, open-ended question.

"I'm fine. I'm taking a vacation."

"In *Las Vegas?*"

"Yes." She didn't bother with an explanation.

"But—" He cleared his throat. "Is Josh being good to you?"

She turned so her back was to the man in question. "Fine."

"I see." He cleared his throat again, and she heard sounds of shifting. "I wanted to say— I mean—" He sighed, his frustration resonating over the phone line. "If you want your job back when your vacation is over, it's yours. We owe you the vacation time. And you'd be damn hard to replace. You're a good businesswoman, Marley."

She closed her eyes. For some reason, the occasional compliment to her business talents failed to suffice this time. It just felt hollow. She didn't respond.

"So— Okay. Why don't you let me talk to Josh again."

"All right. Goodbye."

"Bye, honey." His voice was gruff with impatience.

She handed the phone back, her expression carefully bland.

His gaze briefly probing hers, Josh put the phone to his ear. "Yes?"

Marley turned away, distancing herself from Josh's conversation with her father. She was disoriented enough without having to endure Josh's silent questions.

What was up with her father, anyway? Selling the company he loved to Josh? And now, taking a personal interest in her *emotional well-being?* The father she'd always known would have ranted about responsibility and priorities, and then *bulldozed* over vague or emotional reasoning.

Baffled, she shook her head. She'd more easily understood the last part of their conversation—the business part. They'd always connected smoothly in the workplace. Which brought up another question.

Did she want her old job back? It was a good position, challenging, rewarding, and she was good at what she did. Everything would be so much simpler if she just went back to it. She wouldn't have to hunt for a new job or relocate. Just continue on as though nothing had changed. No risk involved. No adventure necessary.

Hell, just look where her first foray into adventure had landed her: drunk in Las Vegas, and married to a man she didn't even like.

No, that was a lie. She did like Josh, and she really had enjoyed spending today with him. She just didn't know if she could trust him. Heaven only knew what depraved things they'd done last night—things he knew about and she didn't.

Ignoring their most recent kiss, she deliberately recalled a vague memory of his arm against her bare back and satin sheets. She felt again the rush of excitement. But then it fragmented, reemerging as the kiss they'd just shared, and she lost the thread of memory. Damn it. Why couldn't she remember the rest? She glanced over her shoulder, wondering what he remembered that she couldn't.

Had it been good? Had it been fast or slow? Kinky or normal? Had he touched her with his hands, his mouth, his tongue? Her heart began to race. Where had she touched him? She knew his body was hard and strong, had felt that only moments ago for herself. Was he the same olive tone all over, or did he have more vulnerable coloring in places untouched by the sun?

Had she satisfied him?

Somehow, that seemed the most important question right now. If she hadn't, would he still be pursuing her like this? Maybe she *had* satisfied him. Maybe she hadn't been lacking. Or frigid. Still, she'd awakened alone in that bed this morning...

She heard him snap the phone shut.

"Am I frigid?"

The question was out before she could halt the words. *Ugh.* She wanted to die now. Quickly. She felt as vulnerable as a woman standing naked in front of...in front of Josh. The thought completed itself slowly. Still, she had to know. She swallowed heavily and stiffened her spine. "Well? Am I?"

"I heard you the first time, honey." His voice was husky. He moved closer. "You're not frigid. Remember? We already had this discussion."

"So I— So we— Oh, God." She covered her face, remembering the conversation. *A man only accuses a woman of being frigid because he's feeling the sting of his own failure... It's the man's responsibility...and pleasure...to arouse the woman.* Apparently, his expertise had succeeded with her, too. Good Lord, what had she done? What had she let *him* do?

"Marley?"

She shook her head. "This not knowing, this haziness is driving me crazy. I need to remember what happened between us last night."

"Take it easy." He gently took her hands from her face and waited until she looked up at him. "Where's all this coming from all of a sudden? You were fine all day until now."

She shifted her gaze from one place to another, flustered, frustrated, embarrassed, confused... "Maybe it's all just catching up with me. I don't know."

"Are you sure about that?"

She leveled a sharp gaze on him. "What do you mean?"

"Well, if I have to spell it out for you... One minute we're kissing and I'm thinking crazy thoughts. And I think *you're* thinking crazy thoughts. And then your father calls. Next thing I know, you're a mass of insecurities."

She laughed, her chest tight. "I suppose now you're going to turn your philosophical mind to delving through my childhood in search of neuroses. You want to blame this on my relationship with my father."

"I think it might have something to do with it, yes."

"Just *forget* Freud." She fisted her hands. "Put yourself in my place. Suppose *you* were the one who woke up naked and alone in a hotel bed with a wedding ring on your finger. Suppose *you* couldn't remember how you'd gotten there. Suppose *you* couldn't remember sleeping with a woman, didn't know *what* you'd done, *how* you had done it, or even, at first, *who* the woman *was?*" She paused, eyes wide, and let him digest her words.

"Okay." He frowned. "I get it."

"*Do* you? Do you really?"

"Yeah." Restlessly, he turned away from her, paced a few steps, then paced back again. Clasping her shoulders in his big hands, he looked directly into her eyes. "Listen to me. You have nothing—*nothing*—to be ashamed of. You're a beautiful, good-hearted woman with strong ethics and a good head on your shoulders. One night of craziness, after the wallop you received back home, does *not* change that. Got it?"

She reached up, grabbed his wrists, and met his eyes feverishly. "*Then tell me how it was.* What happened last night?"

He didn't respond, but seemed to wrestle with his thoughts. His jaw was tight, his eyes flickering with emotions.

"Damn it, Josh. I could be standing here pregnant with your child and you won't even tell me how I got this way." Her words ended on a hoarse whisper.

He dropped his head, touching her forehead with his. "You're not pregnant, Marley."

She swallowed heavily and ducked to look in his eyes, try to read something there. "So…you used something?"

He lifted his head and met her gaze squarely. "I'm saying I don't make love to women who are too drunk to enjoy the experience. You tempted me almost out of my mind, but no, we did not make love last night."

Marley swayed, a little dizzy, a lot relieved, and a lot—a whole hell of a lot—*angry*. She shoved away from him, speechless for a moment.

He watched her warily.

"You lied."

"Whoa. Stop right there. I didn't lie to you. I never said we slept together. You just assumed—"

"*Wrong*. You *wanted* me to assume it. You never bothered to correct what you *knew* I was thinking."

"Fine. You're right." He grabbed her shoulders again and stared hard into her eyes. "I wanted you. And I wanted you to think of me as a man, not as your father's peon. So, yes. I let you go on thinking whatever you were thinking. If you'd outright *asked* me about it, I wouldn't have lied. But you didn't. Not until now."

"And I suppose that makes it okay."

He stared at her for another frustrated moment before he let his hands drop away. "No, of course it doesn't." He raked a hand through his hair then dropped his hands to his hips. "I'm sorry. I didn't think it would upset you this much. We're not strangers, and you knew even back in Richmond that I was attracted to you. I thought you might be uncomfortable at first with the idea of us together, but I didn't think you'd beat yourself up about it." He paused, then shook his head. "That's all I can say in my defense. I'm sorry."

Reading sincerity in his direct gaze and respect in his quiet words, she couldn't hold on to her anger. She swallowed and folded her arms across her chest. "I guess that explains why I woke up alone."

He nodded silently.

She rubbed her arms, feeling awkward and needing distance. After a lengthy silence, she sighed. "Look, it's late. I want to get up early and see about that divorce."

A frown creased his forehead. He rubbed at it. "I don't suppose you'd consider postponing it for a few days? You just got here. It is your vacation. I hate to see you ruin it already."

She closed her eyes. "I think I know better than to put this off any longer. Fun and adventure seem to mean trouble for me. I'd better get the divorce under way so I can get back to real life before I cause permanent damage."

He touched her shoulder.

She opened her eyes.

"Marley. Please. Don't cut yourself off again. No, you don't have to go wild and fly off to Las Vegas every weekend. But you also don't have to spend your life at the office. Moderation?" He raised his eyebrows. "It is possible to have fun and control at the same time, you know."

"You think?" Her lips twisted. "I haven't seen it yet."

"Oh, Marley." He grinned ruefully and slid an arm around her waist. "Come on. I'll walk you back."

They walked in silence and Marley couldn't help but reflect on the day they'd spent. Josh had fulfilled his promise to give her thrills, screams and fun she'd remember forever. A true adventure. She smiled softly. Even the deception, the wild ups and downs, had been part of it. When all was said and done, she also had to admit she was relieved she hadn't made the huge mistake of sleeping with him while intoxicated. That just felt wrong. She hadn't known him then. She glanced up. She knew him better now. He was so much more than she'd expected.

She thought of his bird, that macaw of romance, and had to chuckle softly.

"What?"

"I'm almost sorry we're leaving so soon. I really liked the idea of my father baby-sitting your talking bird."

He smiled down at her. "You did, huh?" He halted her with a gentle hand on her arm. "Well, he does owe you at least some measure of satisfaction after that deal he made with Larry."

She watched, curious, as he reached into a pocket and pulled out his cell phone.

"Hello, Charles? Josh here again. I need you to do me a favor… Yeah. Look, my bird needs a keeper for the next couple of days while I iron things out here… No, my housekeeper's leaving town tonight. You're all I've got." He glanced at Marley, his eyes twinkling. "No, it's a breeze." He proceeded with a list of instructions for the bird's feeding and care. "Oh, and he needs company. Yeah, visit him and talk to him a lot. If he starts having a shrieking fit, you can also pop in a tape that I keep on top of the TV. Just a show that he likes." He held up a quieting hand when Marley chuckled.

"Hey, if you can't do it, I'll need to come back. The bird's valuable… No, Marley's not ready to come back, and frankly, I'd hate to leave her here alone. So, can you do it?"

Marley heard muffled curses and finally a cranky assent, followed by another curse and a dial tone.

Josh clicked the thing shut and grinned down at her. "Does that help?"

"Immensely." She smiled, relishing just a tiny bit of vengeance. Buy her a fiancé, would he?

Josh frowned. "He won't do anything to traumatize my bird, though, will he?"

"No, of course not." Marley sighed. "He's gruff, but he's not malicious. He'll take care of your bird."

Josh nodded.

Marley frowned. "Lance won't hurt my father, will he?"

"Lance doesn't bite. Your dad'll be okay." Then Josh grinned.

"What?"

"It's just such a domesticated conversation. You'd think we were an old married couple." He grinned down at her.

She rolled her eyes but let the grin tug at her mouth. "Don't push it, buddy."

He left her at her door, and after shutting it behind him, she felt the silence close in on her. She looked around at the luxurious room the maid had tidied for her since she woke up that morning, alone and newly married. It seemed a lifetime ago. She remembered her panic, that awful nausea, the questions, even the naughty excitement.

And Samantha. She picked up the phone and dialed.

"Marley! Finally. I've been worried sick. Where have you been? I've left a dozen messages for you. What's going on?"

Marley plopped down on the magnificent bed,

letting her hand slide across the quilted satin bedspread. "I don't know where to begin."

"How about 'after I hung up the phone this morning…'"

"Okay. After I hung up the phone this morning…" Marley spent the next half hour giving her cousin a replay of her unbelievable day. Samantha laughed over her encounters with the desk clerk, the waiter and the various men she'd approached as possible grooms. Then, as she discussed her adventures with Josh, Sammi held her silence but for a muffled comment or two.

"And so, here I am. I'll be starting the divorce or annulment or whatever tomorrow morning."

"But you didn't sleep with the guy. At all."

"No. He says we didn't and I believe him."

Silence. "Maybe you should have."

"*What?* Are you crazy?"

"No, I'm serious. Don't you hear how you talk about him?"

Marley frowned. "How?"

"Like he's your new boyfriend, you dummy, or maybe a lover you want to take." There was a smile in her cousin's voice.

"Oh, get real, Sammi."

"I *am* real. And don't you wonder how he found you?"

"Now that you mention it, yes."

"I told him where you were."

Marley launched off the bed. "You did *what?*"

"He tracked me down. He was *worried* about you—swore he just wanted to protect you. So I gave him the name of your hotel. Marley, this Josh Walker sounds adorable, and I could tell he really likes you. So I just figured he could be your adventure, all by himself." She chuckled. "And I was right."

"You— Oh, I can't believe—" She was incoherent with fury.

"All right, go ahead and hang up on me, but—"

Marley did. Just plopped the receiver in the cradle like nobody's business. She paced the room, furious. Then she picked up the phone, dialed her cousin and began speaking before the hello had left Sammi's lips. "This is all your doing, then. Josh following me, the wedding, the divorce I need to get. All of it. Some adventure."

Unfazed by her cousin's fury, Samantha just laughed, obviously pleased with herself. "Oh, I think Josh can take some of the credit. A seriously fabulous adventure. I just can't believe you didn't take full advantage of it. And of *him.*"

Samantha paused before continuing, her voice a lilting whisper of temptation. "You still could, you know. You're married, so sex is almost an *obligation.* Someday, you'll look back, see how you flew off to Vegas, married a man in a fit of passion—and then didn't sleep with him. A gorgeous hunk who seems to really care about you." She paused, then continued with quiet certainty. "Don't tell me you wouldn't have regrets."

Marley inhaled sharply, her angry thoughts stumbling to a halt. Lord, she couldn't.

Oh, but Samantha was *right.* She would regret passing this up. She would always wonder. "You are so bad, Sammi." She whispered the words she'd often spoken with laughter. "*So* bad."

"Think about it, Marl. I'll be here." There was a soft click as Samantha broke the connection.

Rattled, Marley set the phone down again. Could she do that? Make love to Josh?

She launched to her feet, paced to the door, back to the bed, paused, retraced her steps. Could she? Would he? Yes. And yes. But *should* she? After ten mi-

nutes of distracted pacing and dithering, Marley just
groaned her frustration and gave up.

She stepped back into the high-heeled mules
she'd kicked off and then stalked determinedly toward the door. Her mind whirling with a confusion
of arousal, anger and trepidation, she decided that
the man still owed her the adventure he'd promised.
The whole adventure, not a partial one that would
leave her with regrets. She was tired of regrets.

She slammed the door behind her, stopped and
glanced down the hallway and back, searching her
memory for his room number.

Suddenly the enormity of what she was doing hit
her. Did she really want to sleep with a man just to
complete her adventure? Could she do that?

No. The realization hit her in a rush. She couldn't
sleep with just any man like that.

But she *could* sleep with Josh. Needed to, wanted
to, *would.* He was under her skin, and, now that she
thought about it, Samantha was right. *Josh* was her
adventure, and she damn well wanted every bit of
him. To hell with doubts.

TWO FLOORS DOWN, Josh frowned into the telephone
while Charles recited his findings and speculations.
None of the pieces seemed to fit and time was running out. Damn it, Marley was going to storm out of
that courthouse tomorrow and fly right back into the
mess they'd left behind them in Virginia.

He sighed, raking his hand through his hair.
"That's all you've got? What about Stan? Did he find
anything else on KTL Consulting in accounting's
files?"

"*No*, damn it. Nothing that doesn't incriminate
Marley."

"There has to be something we're missing." Flipping open his laptop, he called up the files they'd

taken from Marley's computer. He traced a finger down the screen and paused.

The Blaylock project.

He stared. "Charles."

"You find something?"

"Nothing concrete. Hell, there's not much here, but I wonder. Look, I want you to check into something for me." Thinking quickly, Josh ran down a list of instructions and theories.

When he'd finished, Charles grunted thoughtfully.

"It's the only thing that makes sense right now." Josh mentally kicked himself for skipping over newer projects as unlikely. How could he have missed it? This one was Marley's baby—and a brand-new one at that. The timing was right. He just didn't have much to go on with it, and had wasted time analyzing all their existing projects and contractors.

"Hmm." Charles murmured thoughtfully. "You could be on to something there."

"We'd better hope so." Josh pictured the expression on Marley's face should she ever learn what had happened behind her back. It made him feel just a little violent.

"Okay. I'll look into what we have on this, but you know it's still not much to go on. Christ." Charles was murmuring half to himself, obviously troubled still. Then he sighed noisily. "Are you taking care of my daughter?"

Shutting down his laptop, Josh grimaced, his gut tightening again. She didn't deserve any of this. "She's fine. She's tucked away safe in her hotel room now. No thanks to your foolishness."

"Watch your mouth, son. Handshake agreement or no, if I find out you've hurt Marley in any way, you'll never get your hands on my company."

"You wanted to sell me a hell of a lot more than that a few months ago." Remembered anger heated his voice.

"It wasn't like that and you know it."

"What I don't get is why you offered the same deal to Larry. Did you really want him for a son-in-law?"

"Hell, no. But you'd turned me down and I was desperate."

"Maybe. But *she's* not."

"I know. It was a bad plan."

Josh nodded. It was a big admission coming from a man like Charles. "Worse than you know." He lowered his voice. "Some guy's been tailing us. Here in Las Vegas. An older guy, timid. Really bad at shadowing people. I assured Marley that he wasn't one of yours. He's not, is he?"

"Why would I need some incompetent idiot to follow her when I have you down there taking care of her? Hell, no, I didn't hire him—but I'd be willing to bet Larry Donatelli *did*."

Josh sighed. "That's what I figured. Keep an eye on him."

"You can bet on it."

Josh nodded. "So how's my bird?" He heard curses and laughter over the line, and grinned.

"Damn lech. Thought he was making a move on me."

Josh laughed.

"Then I plugged in that tape of yours, and..."

A knock on the door had Josh whipping around. "Hey, Charles, I've got someone at my door. I'll call you tomorrow for an update, okay?"

He hung up and stared at the door. Could it be—

Shaking his head, he went to answer it, and encountered a wide-eyed, nearly angry woman.

"Marley?"

Obviously agitated, she strode past him into his room. "You, Josh Walker, owe me the rest of my adventure."

"I what?" He turned to stare at her, fascinated, as he slowly closed the door behind him.

She faced him, her hands going to the zipper behind her back. "My adventure, remember? I want all of it. I've had my share of exotic drinks, rich food, wild rides and gambling. The only thing I haven't had my fill of—" She slid the zipper down, letting the sequined dress slide to her feet.

"Is *you*."

9

"Me?"

Marley just stared at him, breathless and waiting, hoping. Would he reject her now? Maybe she wasn't sexy enough.

She saw him swallow heavily, his gaze roaming up and down her body, pausing here and there with enough intensity that her fears eased.

He wanted her. *Thank God.*

Taking her courage in both hands, she raised her chin and gave him look for look. "Yes, *you.* I want you, Josh Walker."

He squeezed his eyes shut. She saw his hands tighten into fists he pressed firmly into his own thighs, and then he opened his eyes wide, seeming to fix solely, intently on her face. "Marley. I think this would be a very bad idea right now."

"Oh." So she was mistaken. Wouldn't be the first damned time. With a muffled groan, she closed her own eyes, pondering the least undignified way to pull her dress back up—

"Marley." His voice was a soft caress as he approached her. "You've got it all wrong. My God, I want nothing more in this whole world right now than to take advantage of everything you're offering me. I want you. You know that. I've said it over and over again. Don't doubt it."

With effort, she relaxed her arms at her sides and

stiffened her spine. Whatever he said and did, she would *not* retreat back to the old Marley. Wussy Marley never had any fun. New Marley had *lots* of fun.

She raised her chin. "Then what's the problem? I want you. You want me. We're consenting adults." She forced a sassy grin. "Hell, we're even married. I could probably sue you for cruelty or something if you don't grant me my connubial rights."

That wrung a smile out of him. "I doubt it. But I think you'd have a shot at getting me committed for sheer insanity for not savoring that beautiful body when I had the chance."

"Then savor away." Feeling bold, brazen—and as if she might fall on her face at any moment if he didn't catch her—she approached him.

He seemed to lose the ability to speak. He just stared, his gaze roving over every body part as it moved. Calves, thighs, hips flexing...belly, breasts shifting under lace...then finally, her raised chin and questioning, tempting gaze.

She smiled. Slipping her arms around his neck, she rose on tiptoe, and whispered kisses along his jawline down to his chin. Then she settled, hungrily, on his lips.

He groaned. His hands came to rest on her hips, seemed to grasp with intent, then slacken. Then grasp and firmly set her back from him.

"Josh?" It came out a husky whisper. Would he reject her still? She would just *die*...

"Only a saint could—" He swallowed, audibly.

She waited, heart thumping with nerves, hope and arousal.

"Marley. I can't let you do this now. I just can't. You'll regret it later and hate me for it."

"No, Josh. That was the old Marley. The new one knows what she wants. You. Now."

He shook his head, wordlessly.

"Why?" Knowing he wanted her—she'd felt him hard against her belly, damn it, so there was *no* mistaking—she grew bolder and moved closer. "Come on, Josh. You want me. I want you." She grinned teasingly. "I could add that the vows have even been said. Make love to me."

"But this can't be right for you. Think of everything you've been going through and be honest. What if we weren't married? Would you even consider this? Would you be standing here, wanting this?"

She shook her head, impatient. "But we *are* married. That's not even a factor."

He exhaled with heavy frustration. "But you don't *want* to be married to me. Top of your to-do list tomorrow is seeking out a divorce. Hell, just this morning, you actually threw up when you found out it was *my* ring you were wearing. And now I'm supposed to believe you want to make love with me? Forgive me if I have some doubts." He touched her cheek and smoothed back her hair. His eyes were angry and aroused and concerned. For her.

Her heart turned over. She'd misjudged him so badly. He was such a great guy. The way he'd watched out for her, the laughter they'd shared, the care he'd taken to show her the thrills she'd requested and make her smile. She met his eyes with certainty. "I. Want. You. I want to make love to you. Now. Here. Nothing else matters."

He looked torn.

So she took matters into her own hands. She slid her arms around his neck once more and drew his lips down to hers. Then she opened her heart up and kissed him. She let him feel her affection, her desire, her love of the adventure he'd shown her, and these growing feelings she had for him.

She couldn't deny them. She wasn't the kind of

woman who could sleep with a guy without feeling something for him. She felt. A lot.

Breathing heavily, he released her lips and gazed into her eyes, seeming to look deeply for something he needed.

She waited breathlessly for the verdict, willing to do whatever it took to tip the balance in her favor.

After a moment, he just groaned and smiled.

She smiled back, her arousal building. "Well?"

"Just this." His green eyes were intense. "I am. One *hell* of a lucky man."

"Yes. You are." She raised her eyebrows and gave him a brazen look. "And don't you forget it."

Laughing, he pulled her close and kissed her as if he would never, ever stop. His big hands roamed her back, seeming to pause and memorize the delicate pattern of lace over skin. Then he skimmed them over her upper back and shoulders, and buried his fingers in her hair. As he kissed her, he tunneled his fingers deep in the soft mass, massaging her scalp and eliciting a wordless murmur of approval.

Thrilling over her own boldness, she started nudging him toward the bed that had taunted her since she entered the room.

He budged willingly, taking bigger steps backward until they both toppled, and he rolled to bring her beneath him. His weight pressed her deep into the soft mattress.

The reality of what she was doing buzzed through her thoughts, mingling with excitement and nerves.

"Second thoughts?" He seemed to expect them, his eyes already dimming with disappointed acceptance.

"Are you so willing to quit, then?" It was a taunting question, driven by bravado and arousal.

"It might be the end of me, but for you, I might—"

"Just you *try* stopping." She gave him a bold stare. "And I guarantee that it *will* be the end of you."

He laughed in husky relief, then lowered his gaze to take in the bustier she'd spent long minutes adjusting before their evening on the town.

Seeing his rapt stare, she grinned. "You like?"

"Oh, damn right I like." He met her gaze with lurid curiosity. "Is this the kind of thing you wear to work every day under those sensible suits?"

She gave him a teasing smirk. "And if I said yes?"

He swallowed hard, his eyes desperately earnest. "If I'd known, I'd have worn a boner to every meeting."

She laughed up at him.

"I'm not kidding. You'd have been the end of my career. I had a hard enough time concentrating when I thought you were wearing simple white cotton."

She pressed her lips together, refusing to admit that she *had* worn that white cotton.

He gave her a shrewd, laughing look. "You fake. You do not wear this stuff to work every day."

She raised her eyebrows, bluffing. "Who says?"

"I do."

She grinned. "Well. I think I'll have to change my ways then. Cotton goes in the trash can tomorrow morning."

"So you're going on a spending spree at the lingerie store?" He gave her an intrigued look before running a finger down her throat and into her cleavage. "Can I watch?"

She caught her breath. "Yes."

"When?"

"When I can afford it."

At his knowing smile, she gave him a bold look. "White cotton *still* goes in the trash tomorrow, though. Until I can restock, I guess I'll just have to…go without."

His eyes seemed to glaze over. "Death. By chronic boner."

She laughed.

He groaned. "I've wanted you like this for so long. Hot and hungry for me." He bent to nip at the tendon in her neck, pausing to blow on the flesh before sampling another taste farther down.

She gasped at the sting, shifting restlessly beneath teasing lips and fingers. "Then *do* something about it. It's rude to make a girl wait."

He chuckled at her impatience, his eyes glowing with his own arousal. Then he *did* something about it, dipping beneath a lacy cup to free her breast for his undivided attention. Soon he had her twisting on the mattress, arching her back and freeing the other breast. He kissed and drew it deep into his mouth.

She arched again and groaned impatiently, wanting to be free of her lacy restrictions.

Helping hands slid around her rib cage, tingling nerve endings along the way, and met behind her back.

Where he fumbled, dropped his head to her neck, and cursed.

She laughed breathlessly.

He raised his head, looking pained. "Whoever designed this thing is sadistic. How does it come off?" After a lengthy, teasing search, he finally found the fastenings running from cleavage to midriff and freed her—one tiny button at a time.

Pausing in the act of tossing it aside, he studied the bustier with a bewildered grin.

She just laughed, plucked it out of his hand and flipped it onto the floor. Then, purposefully, she reached for the buttons of his shirt, working at them until his chest was bare. He shrugged his arms free and she let her hands slide over his shoulders then down over his chest and ribs. Her gaze was blatantly admiring. His chuckle ended on a gasp as she rose to nip and tease her way down his neck and across his chest, her hands busily working their way lower.

"Speaking of sadistic—" he teased hoarsely and gasped again, nearly mindless at the feel of her hands on him. Hell, he'd expected shy passion from Marley, but the playful aggression was a welcome surprise. He grinned, completely enchanted, then grabbed those mischievous hands of hers, firmly clasping them around his neck.

She flashed him a wicked smile then lowered her lashes to peer through them at him. "You keep looking at me that way."

Resting on an elbow, he let one hand drift caressingly over her breasts, enjoying the voluptuous pleasure of curving flesh. "What way?"

Her gaze flickered as his fingers drifted lower, seeking out sensitive hollows beneath her ribs. "Like you're trying to figure something out."

He smiled, his gaze still on hers as he let his fingers glide lower. He circled and dipped into her navel before dwelling on ticklish hollows near her hipbones.

She squirmed, torn between escape and enjoyment.

"I am trying to figure something out. You."

He caressed deliberately lower.

"What pleases you. What teases you."

He slid the panties off her, brushing lightly across everything in their wake. She gasped.

He smiled. "What drives you wild."

He caressed more boldly, the feel of slick heat almost more than he could bear.

"I want to know...*everything*."

She cried out and arched her back, exposing the length of her throat for his lips, the scrape of his teeth. His fingers ruthlessly sought her pleasure, caressing boldly and lightly, the rhythm a torturously varied thing. As her cries grew more demanding, so did his hands and his mouth.

"Oh, Josh. *Enough.* You're driving me crazy."

"Good." He yanked open a nightstand drawer and fumbled for a condom. Hungry—desperate almost— with her long legs sliding restlessly open and winding with welcome around his hips, he was finally ready.

He groaned and briefly closed his eyes. His breathing heavy, he surrendered to a deep-seated need that overrode even the physical one. "Marley, look at me."

Her breath came in gasps and her eyes were unfocused.

"*Look at me.* I want you to see me and tell me you want me. I don't want to be just some crazy adventure for you. *Tell me you want me.* Now."

She swallowed convulsively, her legs tight around his waist. Still, she concentrated. Desperately. On him. "I want you. *Please*, Josh." The last was half plea, half command, and ended on a gasp as he surged deeply inside.

The man was *endowed.*

She gasped, squirming slightly to adjust. Wow. And it had been so long—

He dropped his forehead to the hollow in her neck, panting like a long-distance runner in his effort to slow the driving need of his body.

After a long moment, he began moving slowly, carefully. Perspiration shone on his forehead, and his jaw worked almost viciously. Josh was obviously being careful no matter how much it hurt him. He was holding back. And the faint, teasing pleasure was killing her. Slowly. As was her impatience.

Finally, she reached up and fisted her hands in his hair, forcing him to meet her eyes. He looked a little dazed.

"If you don't get on with it, I'll be forced to do something drastic." Her words were measured, her eyes fierce.

"Yeah?" A wondering grin spread across his face, despite his obvious frustration.

So be it. She lowered her lashes and dragged his mouth down to hers, her lips and tongue feverishly seeking his. As he sank into her kiss, ran wild with it, she tightened her legs around his waist and arched upward, taking him deep.

The breath whooshed from his lungs. *Drastic is good.*

Then his body took over in a demanding rhythm that drove him beyond every thought save one. She was his now—her body shuddered beneath him, as he lost his own battle for control—and he wouldn't let her go.

The sounds of their cries still echoed in his ears when Josh found the strength to lever himself to the side. He tugged her close.

She sprawled limp across his chest, her body still trembling with aftershocks. He soothed her with caressing touches and light kisses on her temple, but she kept her face buried in his neck.

After a few moments, Josh excused himself briefly. When he returned to the bed, Marley was curled in a ball under the satin covers, apparently sound asleep.

Josh frowned. He'd intended having a frank talk with her, assuming he could find the right words. Granted, that was one hell of an assumption. There were no right words. Impatience gnawed at him. Everything was still unsettled between them.

Still, maybe the timing was off. It had been a long day for Marley. Thinking over events of the past twenty-four hours, he couldn't help a rueful grin. It was no wonder she was exhausted.

Flipping off the lights, he climbed under the covers and pulled her into his arms. God, but he could get used to the feel of her against him in the night. The woman was one surprise after another, and just thinking about her most recent demands made him horny as a teenager all over again.

Grinning, he ducked to bury his nose in the fragrant auburn mass at his shoulder. Smelling that elusive scent, the one that had teased him these past few months and now would linger on his pillow come morning, he let possessiveness surge through him. She was his. She might not acknowledge it yet, but she was his.

His job, he supposed, was to coax Marley into realizing—and admitting—the depths of *her* feelings for *him*. No easy task, but it should be quite an adventure.

FEELING THE RAYS of sunlight prying at her closed eyelids, Marley groaned and turned onto her stomach. She slid her naked arms beneath her pillow and cuddled its softness to her cheek. Sighing, she squirmed just a little, the bare skin of her legs and belly sliding against satiny sheets. The cool material felt good against tiny aches here and there. And there.

The sensations registered. She froze, afraid to open her eyes. Déjà vu. Wait. Maybe it had all been a dream, or…maybe she was in Richmond and she'd never left… Heart pumping feverishly with either hope or disappointment, she opened her eyes.

And stared into lazy green ones. Sleep-tousled dark hair, a satisfied grin—and lots of hard, olive-toned flesh.

God, he was beautiful.

"Morning, sleepyhead." Josh's voice was morning husky and tenderly amused.

She licked her lips, trying to reorient herself. Unemployed. Las Vegas. Rum punches and wedding vows? *Sex.* Glorious, sweaty, oh-my-God-it-was-good sex. Yes. But now… She tried for breezy sophistication. "Good morning." She couldn't believe…did she *really* do all those things…?

He reached out to tuck a lock of hair behind her ear, then covered the fist she'd clenched around the corner of her pillow. He caressed her hand, a gentle coaxing.

Carefully, she relaxed her grip.

"Are you okay?" He spoke quietly, his gaze direct.

"Sure. Why wouldn't I be?" Discreetly, she tugged at the sheet, trying to cover more of her bare back and the sides of her naked breasts.

He ignored her attempts at modesty. "I could tell it had been a while for you. And we went a little crazy last night."

Inwardly, she groaned. *You could say that again.* She'd been aggressive, demanding, shameless, irresponsible. And had positively *reveled* in it. All of it. She'd never been that way with a man before. Ever. Her heart thudded with sick uncertainty. "I'm fine."

"Okay." But those green eyes saw too much. They understood, didn't demand, just…knew. Somehow, that was even more alarming. "How about breakfast?" he asked softly.

"Sure." She cleared her throat. "Um, just let me use your bathroom a minute. Can I take a shower?" She needed distance.

"Of course." He smiled, his eyes intimate. He looked for all the world like a patient predator—watching, waiting, confident of the eventual outcome. At this rate, *hell,* he was probably right. Give her ten minutes and she'd lose all shame and joyfully jump him again. Her barriers and defenses had all come tumbling down and he was irrevocably *in.*

Not that that was necessarily a *bad* thing. It could be a wonderful thing. She just hadn't expected to feel so damned vulnerable to him.

Oh, God. Shower. Privacy. Now. *Regroup, regroup.* "Thanks." She sat up, awkwardly pulling the sheet around her. As she stood up, he rose along with her, unconscious of his nakedness as he helped her secure the sheet around her body.

"Room's kind of cold, huh?" He smiled down at her, loosely embracing her from behind. He was even offering her an excuse so she could gracefully cover up if that's what she needed.

Panic completely set in. The man was perfect. Intelligent, affectionate, mannerly, funny, strong, and oh, God, sexy as hell in the morning. She hadn't planned on this. She wasn't supposed to feel so much. It was supposed to be an adventure, right? Something to savor after it was over. How had things changed so much? When had affection and friendship grown so alarmingly?

She swallowed the sudden lump in her throat, gesturing vaguely as she pulled free of his arms. "I'll just, um…"

"Take your time, honey. I'll order breakfast." He traced a finger down her cheek, touching the corner of her mouth. The skin there was tender from repeated kisses. And caresses. And—

Gripping the sheet tightly, she walked as casually as she could toward the bathroom. Still, it probably looked like the all-out retreat it really was. She closed the door with relief.

Hesitantly, she turned toward the mirror over the sink, not crazy about the idea of facing it right now. When she glimpsed her reflection, she couldn't help but stare. That woman…was her? She reached out a trembling hand, touched the mirror and drew back. Her hair tumbled wildly about her shoulders, smashed flat on one side where she'd slept. Sure, it was a mess, but the unnerving part was the look in her eyes. She looked well kissed, well used. Well loved.

Flinching from that last idea, she turned the tap on and used a bar of soap to scrub away at the remnants of makeup on her face. She was being ridiculous. Unsophisticated. So she and Josh hooked up last night. Big deal. Women around the world did it these days. Hell, she was the one who'd initiated the encounter. So maybe the reality had exceeded her lascivious expectations. That was cause for celebration not regression.

After all, the whole idea behind this trip was to leave wussy, rational Marley back in Richmond and cut loose a little. Be adventurous. And last night had been long on adventure and short on restraint. So she was allowed to be a little nervous—as long as she didn't cave to those nerves. And she wouldn't.

Resolved and calmer now, Marley turned to dry her face on the hand towel when she heard a metallic pinging sound.

A glint of gold caught her eye and she focused on a ring—the wedding ring—where it lay on the floor. After resisting all of yesterday's twisting and tugging, a little soap and water today had the ring literally falling off her finger.

She studied it for a moment, at a loss. Then, silently, she picked it up and slid it back onto her finger.

She stared at the tiny diamond sparkling on her hand. What was she doing? It had come off—finally—and here she was sliding the damn thing back on? *Why*, for heaven's sake?

Involuntarily, she remembered that waiting, affectionate look in Josh's eyes. She blinked it away. She'd just keep the ring safe for him until their marriage was dissolved. What safer place than on her finger? She'd give it to him after their visit to the courthouse.

OUTSIDE, JOSH WAITED until he heard the shower running before picking up the phone again. He'd ordered breakfast moments ago, and now he had another call to make.

"Charles. Josh here."

An explosive sigh echoed over the phone lines.

"Damn. I guess that's my update."

"If you mean *no* update, then yes, it is." Charles's angry frustration mirrored Josh's feelings as well. "I can't find the damn files, but I'm working on it. What about you? Anything?"

Josh glanced at his laptop, his gut tightening. "I haven't had a chance to work on it since last night. But listen. I have to tell Marley what's been going on."

"Damn it, you can't. I don't have enough yet. Just give me a little more time to—"

"But I *have* to tell her. Things have gone too far. I—" Josh halted, aware he was on the verge of revealing too much.

The silence told him he already had.

"Where's my daughter, Josh?"

"I'm taking care of her."

"Define 'taking care of,'" Charles growled.

"I care about your daughter. I won't hurt her."

"Damn straight you won't."

"Understood."

There was a moment of silence while Charles digested the respectful tone offered by a man seriously interested in his daughter. "All right then. I suppose I…could be pleased about this. Assuming your intentions—"

Josh laughed without humor. "God, no, Charles. Do *not* approve. Not after the fiasco with Larry. That would be the end of any chance I might have with your daughter. Try ignorance. That might work. Hell, we have enough challenges ahead without your 'help' and 'approval.'"

There was no turning back now. He could only hope that what he and Marley had begun yesterday and last night, would be strong enough to outlast what was ahead of them.

He'd extracted promises from her, too, little did she know it. She'd admitted she wanted him regardless of their marital status, *regardless* of her need for adventure. He was determined to keep their attraction to each other separate from all that.

"Fine then. But you hurt my daughter and you'll damn well pay for it." Charles's voice was certain.

"Well, she's *going* to be hurt. There's no way around it." Josh fisted a hand in frustration. "Damn it, I've been keeping things from her. She's not going to like it."

Charles let out a gusty sigh. "A month ago, I'd have argued with you. She's always been a practical, reasonable little thing. But I just don't know anymore. The way she flew off the handle about Donatelli... Hell, why didn't you settle things with her up here before you left? Or wait until you come back?"

"*You're* the reason she's down here at all."

"You think I don't know that?" Charles bit off a curse. "Everything's a mess right now. I screwed up. I'm just relieved as hell she's not here to witness how bad it's all gotten. Gossip, investors balking, clients questioning...hell."

"Yeah, well the worst of it is going to be when she finds out her ex-fiancé is responsible for framing her. Right now she just thinks he's a greedy idiot—not an embezzler hip deep in organized crime and looking to take her down in his place."

"Hell."

"I'll second that. Look, I have to go. Expect us back in town sometime in the next day or two. I don't think I can keep her here much longer. See how much tail you can chase between now and then, would you?"

"You're acting pretty damn cocky for a man who doesn't own my company yet." Charles's voice lowered in warning. "*Or* my daughter. You screw up and I'll break this deal, I swear it. Watch yourself with Marley."

10

GUILT RIDING HIM, Josh stared hard out the window. What Charles didn't know was that Josh had already screwed up. And honestly, he wouldn't change a minute of last night if he had it to do all over again. The woman could tempt a saint, and Lord knew he was anything but.

The bathroom door opened and Marley stepped out. She wore a fluffy white robe with the hotel's name embroidered on the pocket—and nothing else under it, he'd be willing to bet. Her hair was wet and slicked straight back from her face, but for a curl fighting its way loose at her temple.

She wore no makeup and no jewelry except the ring he'd given her. He looked at it, remembering. His mother had given him her wedding ring as a memento after his father's death and her remarriage. In a way, he'd seen it as her goodbye to love and to a life of risk she couldn't handle.

He'd felt awkward at the time, not sure what to do with the damn thing, but he'd kept it close because it felt vaguely as if he should. As a reminder, perhaps, that he needed to fulfill something. Maybe succeed where his own father had screwed up.

For years, Josh had worn it on a chain around his neck—until the night before last, when he'd slipped it on Marley's finger. It looked amazingly right on her hand. It was small, true, but its simplicity looked elegant on her slender fingers.

If she'd just give him a chance, he'd give her the love and promises and adventures that his own mother had forfeited—and see to it that Marley never regretted her trust in him.

When Marley slipped her hand into a pocket of the robe and shifted a little self-consciously, he realized he'd been staring and smiled. "Damn. Why do women even bother with makeup? You come in wearing nothing but a robe and play absolute hell with my head and my body. You're beautiful, Marley."

She smiled back, seemed almost shy all of a sudden. Not a big surprise—he was almost certain the whole morning-after scenario wasn't a situation she encountered often. She gestured toward the door. "Did I hear room service?"

"That you did. Let's feed you."

"You seem to do that a lot." Her smile relaxing into a genuine grin, she joined him at the table in his room. They ate quietly, with Marley lost in thought and Josh watchful.

"What's up, Marley? You've hardly said a word. Do you regret last night?"

She took a moment to set down her fork and wipe her lips with a napkin. "No." She spoke hesitantly at first, then smiled and met his eyes. "No, I don't regret it at all."

"Excellent." He flashed her a wicked grin, a quick glance at the bed forecasting where his thoughts lay.

Oh, she was tempted. But no. "I don't regret *last* night…but the night *before* last is another matter." She cleared her throat. "I'm going to the courthouse this morning to get our marriage dissolved. Just as soon as I get clothes from my room and do something with all of this." She gestured sheepishly toward her hair and fresh-scrubbed face.

"You already know my opinion on the 'all this.'" He smiled briefly. "But do you really have to go to

the courthouse so soon? I wouldn't mind spending
a lazy morning with you wearing nothing but that
robe."

"I can't, Josh." She spoke quietly. "I need to take
care of the divorce as soon as possible. We did everything out of order, and that just doesn't work for
me." She shrugged and gave him a wry look. "I'm
trying to play nice with my rational side."

"I guess that makes sense." He sounded reluctant, as though he wanted to say more.

Of course he did. She smiled. *He felt something, too.*
"But Josh? After the divorce…"

His eyebrows rose.

"I want to keep seeing you."

"Well, *thank God* for that." He smiled, eyes twinkling.

"Tonight, after everything is settled, legally, we'll
just be a normal couple spending time together. Getting to know each other. And we can see where it
goes from there." She gave him a searching look.
"All right?"

"Okay." He seemed to struggle with the idea. "But
Marley, at least let me go with you to the courthouse
this morning."

Puzzled, she shook her head mildly. "Well, yeah.
Don't you have to be there? To divorce me?"

He blinked. "Oh. Yeah, you're right. Just let me get
dressed and I'll walk you back to your room to get
some clothes. Then we'll go together."

TWO HOURS LATER, Marley stalked out of the courthouse building, her frustration palpable. For his own
part, Josh could feel nothing but weak relief. A reprieve. He'd sort of suspected, but… He held his silence while Marley ranted.

"I can't believe it. Of all the irresponsible, bait-
and-switch tactics. So, you can fly to Las Vegas, get

drunk out of your mind and be wed before the clock strikes midnight. But a divorce the next day when you're sober? *Oh,* no. You have to be a Nevada *resident* for that. Of all the nerve." She paced back and forth. "And they were open *yesterday.* I could have learned this *yesterday,* maybe even started proceeding to reverse the situation." She groaned ignoring what she might have missed otherwise. Her adventure with Josh. No, she couldn't resist yesterday. Maybe she should, but she didn't want to. "Well, there's no help for it. We'll fly back to Richmond tonight and start proceedings in the morning."

Josh's mood took a nosedive. This was worse than he'd expected. "You want to fly back to Richmond *tonight?*"

"Yes." She glanced at him. "I'm sorry, Josh. I know we had plans tonight, but this can't wait any longer. I've been irresponsible long enough. I'm booking the next flight home."

Unfortunately, the next flight to Richmond wasn't until the next day and Marley—still unemployed and currently draining her bank account—paid an absolute mint for the ticket. She grimaced. If she hadn't been so taken with the idea of buying a one-way ticket to Las Vegas, she already would have a return ticket to Richmond. Given the past few days, and now this, did she need any more evidence that she wasn't cut out for a life of risk and adventure?

But did she regret yesterday's adventures? Last night's?

Reluctantly, she smiled, and she knew it was a goofy expression. Oh, no. Last night had been more than worth the hassle. Josh had made her feel more wildly feminine than at any other time in her life. That experience, that feeling, was priceless.

"Marley?" Josh smiled quizzically, discreetly waving his fork to get her attention.

"Hmm?" She smiled up at him. The sounds and smells of the hotel restaurant returned to focus.

"Where were you?"

"I was just thinking that this trip wasn't a total washout."

His eyebrows rose. "That's good, I guess. Considering you've spent most of it with me." He grinned at her.

She laughed and stabbed delicately at the salad she'd ordered for lunch.

"It's lucky for you that I have such a strong self-image."

She rolled her eyes at his angelic expression. "Try cocky. I bet you believe all those things Lance tells you over breakfast. 'Oh, Sirena. I'm not worthy. You deserve better than to wallow in the putrid refuse of my life.'" She grinned at the image of a bird perched on Josh's shoulder, squawking sweet disgustings in his ear.

"Saw that episode, did you?" Josh's smile was lopsided.

Marley nearly choked on a tomato slice. Still coughing and laughing, she shook her head. "I have got to meet this bird."

"So why don't you?" He spoke casually, but in his eyes she could see memories of the night before. And the promise of more.

"So why don't I?" She smiled, her gaze drawn to and held by his. "I meant what I said this morning. After we get this marriage dissolved, I'd like to see you again. Away from all this fantasy."

"I want that, too. But Marley." He regarded her seriously. "Not all of this has been fantasy. Last night was real. What you and I have together is real."

She smiled wistfully at him, still wrestling with her own doubts, her own reality. "Is it? Last night was so special, and I swear I don't regret it. I'm glad it happened. But…"

"But?"

"I just don't know if it's more than that. Not yet. I mean, in case you haven't noticed, I haven't been acting like myself since I found out my father bought me a fiancé."

"Is that why you're in such a rush to undo what happened your first night here?" His gaze probed hers. "You're doubting all the decisions you've made since the argument with your father?"

"Well, that first night, certainly. Come on, Josh. I was so drunk I don't even remember our wedding. That says something, don't you think? And, having known me these past few months, can you honestly say anything I did that night sounds like something I would normally do?" She shook her head. "Singing in bars, dancing on tables, the bar brawl, *everything*."

He smiled briefly, memories flashing in his eyes. "It depends. Sometimes I don't think you know yourself very well. Not all of you. You know the controlled, competent Marley. The rational Marley who makes her father proud. What about the woman I made love to last night? She was real. And she was you."

That gave her pause, but she shook it off nonetheless. "I don't regret last night. And I won't deny that last night had potential for more. But I was acting on impulse at the time and, frankly, I don't usually make decisions that way. If we're talking about a relationship, something more than just a vacation fling…" She frowned, uncertain.

"You think every decision has to be planned well in advance for it to be a good one?" He smiled at her, his forehead wrinkled.

"Well, until recently, that's how I made all my decisions. At least, all the big ones."

"And were they all good decisions?"

Again he threw her. "No. Not all. My engagement was a monumentally *bad* decision, for example."

He grinned. "And I was an impulsive, monumentally *good* decision."

She laughed. "Nothing wrong with *your* ego. Despite the beating you say I give it. But, sure, I'll go along with that."

"Good." He picked up his fork. "So what do you say we devote the rest of today...and tonight...to impulse."

Watching his fingers deftly work the fork, she felt her stomach flutter. She knew exactly how she'd like to spend the rest of the day and night. Before facing Richmond tomorrow.

God, but she wanted him. He'd stopped eating to stare at her again. She licked suddenly dry lips. His gaze dropped to her mouth. Newly liberated hormones tangoed all over her resolve...

Josh dropped his fork and signaled the waiter for the check.

"I hadn't intended—" she began.

"I know." His gaze never left hers. "But it's such a monumentally *good* impulse."

"I guess we are stuck here for the night, after all." Her voice bobbled the words; her tongue and throat couldn't seem to coordinate properly.

He grinned, slow and sexy. "There you go, stroking my ego again."

He signed the receipt and hauled her out of her chair.

Giddy and breathless, she let him lead her across the lobby and onto the elevator. As the doors closed, she turned to stare at him, feeling like an animal in heat. Possessive and reveling in it, too. *So* un-Marley. She let the thought dwindle. Let all mental functioning cease, except—

"Marley, unless you want to give everyone on the

next floor an eyeful, you've got to stop looking at me like that."

Catching her breath, she glanced away, flushed and self-conscious. She was *so* out of her depth.

He tugged her chin around until she met his hot gaze. "Stop that. I've wanted to see that look in your eyes for months. I just never expected you to pack this much punch. It's making me nuts." He grinned slowly. "I want you naked."

The elevator doors opened and a couple stepped in, laughing and talking.

Josh never took his eyes off Marley, and she couldn't take her eyes off him. She was very much afraid he could read everything she was thinking and feeling, and *oh* my, but the things she was imagining. Him, naked and hungry. She let her lips curve slightly, watched his pupils dilate.

She wanted to be on top this time.

The elevator doors opened.

Josh grabbed her hand, hauled her down the corridor and into his room. The slam of the door still echoed in their ears as he took her mouth with a hungry groan. His hands slid all over her body, yanking on buttons. One popped and flew across the room. Her hands joined his and more buttons popped. She just laughed against his mouth until his lips slid down her throat—and sucked the tip of her bared breast deep inside his mouth.

Her laugh broke off on a high-pitched cry. Her knees weakened and she slid a few inches down the door, but he caught her under the arms and held her fast. He licked at the underside of her breast one last time before nipping his way to her ribs and lower. She flinched. When she would have pulled his head up to hers, he grinned and dropped to a knee.

Still holding her against the door, he bunched her

skirt with the other hand until it rode above her hips. Then he glanced below it and paused. Significantly.

Her breath uneven, her heart shuddering, she couldn't find her voice to speak.

"No white cotton?" He sounded hoarse.

Utterly naked below the waist and feeling just the slightest bit drafty, she offered him what she hoped was a brazen smile.

"If I'd known you were naked under that skirt— At the *courthouse,* even." He looked a little shocked, a whole lot impressed and turned on as hell.

"It could even be a misdemeanor?" she offered shakily.

"Honest to God, you are the most amazing woman."

And he continued to *look.* She felt his breath on her and goose bumps rose. So painfully, arousingly intimate. She couldn't catch a steady breath. His gaze didn't waver, his breath coming faster as he drew nearer.

He wasn't— Surely he wasn't going to—

Oh, but he *was.* And she was torn between wanting it desperately and desperately not wanting it, and…oh, wow.

With his tongue, he traced a line from her navel, down, slowly. She grabbed at his hair, but he didn't alter his course, just drew inevitably closer, and then he was *there.*

And then her knees did buckle.

But it only made his way easier. Bracing her with his free arm and shoulder, he took full advantage, tormenting and pleasuring like a man who knew way too damn much about a woman's body. The man was criminally proficient. Release took her by force, and she arched mindlessly over him, boneless and shuddering.

He caught her and gently lowered her to a soft rug

on the floor. Then she looked up into his eyes, and the intensity in them sent her pulse skittering back up. Hands and arms tangled, yanking at his clothing and the rest of hers.

When he was naked and ready for her, she pulled him close, felt his heart thundering in his chest. For her. She met his eyes again and saw only green fire. His face was taut with it.

She stared, wonderingly, at him. Had a man ever wanted her this much? Cool, controlled Marley? No, never.

"Incredible." She little more than mouthed the word.

He flashed a wicked grin. "Why, thank you."

She laughed, a breathless croaking. But it energized her enough that she gave his shoulder a push. Reluctantly, he gave over, his gaze watchful and hungry as he rolled onto his back.

She came down on top of him, parting her knees to hug his hips between them. There, she hovered, just short of paradise. When he would have lunged upward to take her, she inhaled sharply and flexed her thighs to hold him still.

"Tease." It was a husky accusation, his eyes laughing and hot.

"No. *Pilates.*" She grinned, feeling a little silly and wild and drunk on feminine power. The she eased herself slowly, torturously downward.

Groaning, he clamped his hands on her hips and urged her into a frantic rhythm that rocketed them both to a hard climax. Her legs weak like jelly, she slumped onto him, burying her face into his neck.

He rubbed her back gently and kissed the top of her head. After a moment, he started chuckling.

"What?" The word was muffled against his neck.

"I wish you weren't so damn frigid and rational all the time, woman."

She laughed weakly. "It's your fault. You do this to me."

"Good." The word rumbled from his chest.

Later, as they lolled in the pool-size bathtub together, drinking champagne while bubbles frothed all around them, she was forced to agree.

"I like this." She rolled her head lazily on the back of the tub, feeling like a contented cat while he rubbed the arches of her feet. Every once in a while, he'd slide a hand up to cup the calf of her leg or gently stroke her thigh until she gasped. He was teasing and possessive and she loved every minute of it. It also didn't hurt that she could study that marvelous naked chest of his at her leisure. Or slide a foot gently over the submerged portions of his body.

"Mmm. I see that." He grinned at her. He dug a knuckle into the ball of her foot and she groaned, shamelessly.

Lazy and content in their intimacy, she let her thoughts rule her words. "I really like how I am with you."

"I like it, too. But it's not more of this fantasy stuff you were spouting earlier, is it?" He spoke in a lazy hush that removed any provocation from his words.

"I don't know. Maybe, maybe not."

"Know what I think?"

"Hmm?" She gasped, distracted. "Oh, there, yes."

Smiling, he kneaded her calf until she groaned. "I think this is the woman you are when you let your guard down. You just don't do it very often."

She closed her eyes. "Maybe."

"More than maybe. When's the last time you let work and Brentwood Electronics leave your mind for any length of time? When's the last time you just let yourself be Marley?"

"Around my cousin."

"Who else? Anyone?"

She thought. Opened her eyes to meet his. "I don't know. No one, I guess." *You*.

"It's always been just you and your father, right?"

"No sibs. And my mom died when I was little. So, yes, just Dad and me." She half shrugged. "Well, and Samantha, too, but that's a little different."

He nodded, thoughtful. "Do you and your father do stuff together? What do you talk about?"

"Work."

"Anything else? Memories?"

She shrugged. "He's not the sentimental type."

"What about that ex-fiancé of yours? What did you discuss with him besides work and goals?"

She met his questions with silence.

"So you're Marley the businesswoman with him, too." He spoke slowly, as though fitting pieces together. "Don't you think it's possible that you've let Marley the businesswoman take the lead for so long, that you wouldn't even recognize yourself as just a woman with just a man?"

"I suppose it's possible." Sitting up, she gently tugged her foot free and sipped at her champagne. "What's your point?"

Reaching across, he plucked the champagne out of her hands and sipped lightly at the spot on the glass that was still moist from her lips. He held her gaze. "The point is, this thing between you and me is no fantasy. It's just unfamiliar to you. That doesn't make it any less real. We're real."

She stared. Was it possible? Heaven knew she hadn't faked a moment of their lovemaking. And the laughter was real enough. Maybe there was something to what he was saying. She hoped.

He handed the champagne glass to her, his eyes warm and intimate. She took the glass, her eyes still on his, and sipped where he'd sipped, watching his eyes grow darker.

He reached for her and she dropped the glass in the tub as she reached right back. Champagne bubbles mixed with scented ones and by the time they'd finished with each other, there was slippery water all over the floor and rug.

Sweeping her into his arms, Josh laughed down at the boneless heap of woman he'd rescued from near disaster on a slick floor. He hauled her into the bedroom, tossed her playfully on the huge bed and dropped down with her.

She reached for him.

"*Again?* You're insatiable, woman. Give me time to recover. I think I've got swimmer's ear from the last time. You know you damn near let me drown while you had your way with me."

She giggled and curled up with him. Honestly giggled. Marley Brentwood. Giggling. Lying sopping wet in bed in a luxury hotel room. With a man. It was absolutely delicious, she decided, content against his chest.

And every bit of it was her. He was right. She owed him for that, she decided, letting her mind drift off into dreams.

Watching her fall asleep, Josh smiled to himself. Wasn't the male supposed to fall asleep while the female insisted on pillow talk? Leave it to Marley to defy the stereotype. Just another piece in this puzzle that kept growing in complexity.

As did his feelings for her. And the situation in which he found himself. His grin faded.

It was one thing to tell lies to a woman in order to protect her; quite another to lie to a lover in order to steal more time with her.

WHEN MARLEY WOKE NEXT, it was dark. A glance at the clock told her it was two in the morning. And she was, once again, naked between satin sheets. She seemed to be making a habit of this. Except she was nowhere near upset about it this time. In fact, she might just have to buy a set of satin sheets for her own bed. Enjoying the thought, she turned her head on the pillow to look at the man still sleeping next to her.

He was frowning. Unlike hers had been, his dreams must be less than pleasant. In that case, she decided, he probably wouldn't mind being awakened from them. She slid closer and let her lips trail lightly over his face. He seemed to lean into her touch, and his expression eased. She smiled and settled her lips on his mouth, kissing and nibbling gently until he responded. She deepened the kiss, feeling a rush of that lovely power.

Until Josh, she'd never suspected she might have that kind of impact on a man. It was heady. Addictive. Smiling against his lips, she slid her hands over his body, seeking.

Groaning, he leaned into her kiss, and his hips rocked forward, seeking her. Finding her. Their loving was slow and warm, erotic in the denial inherent in their pacing. They wanted but controlled; desired but delayed. For now. Her breath came in low gasps that complemented the raggedness of his breathing and his slow, deliberate thrusts. They slow-rocked each other to tender but monumental climax.

"I love you." She whispered the words as her shudders eased. It was a gentle realization, if a sudden one for her. She knew it was true, though. Marley Brentwood, with her patience and her control and her rational planning, had flown to Las Vegas, married a man she hardly knew, then fallen in love with him, all in just a few days' time.

It was monumentally irrational. And yet, so real.

"I do, Josh." She looked directly into his eyes. "I

love you." She smiled, feeling joyfully reckless. "Forget the divorce. Let's honeymoon in Vegas. For real this time."

Just saying the words was thrilling. What she'd found with Josh was crazy and wonderful and perfect. How had she lucked into something as beautiful and real as love? She laughed aloud. Luck? What was she thinking? She was in Vegas, for heaven's sake. The city *thrived* on luck, and everything was a gamble.

She won.

HE LOST.

He'd gambled big, won more than he'd expected—and now he could very well lose everything.

"I love you, too, Marley. So much. You have to believe that." He stared at her, willed her not to hate him. He watched her jubilation fade as she realized there was a "but" in there, and it was coming up right about now—

"But we're not married. We never were."

11

MARLEY STARED, speechless for a moment, then just shook her head. *"What?"* She pulled her left hand from beneath the covers. "This is your ring."

"Yes." He traced the diamond solitaire and gold band, then met her eyes. "And I want you to keep wearing it and marry me for real if you'll still have me. God, I want that more than anything in the world. But we're not married. Not yet."

She pulled away, wide-eyed and stunned. "You're joking."

"I wish. But no. I'm serious." When she slid out of the bed, taking the sheet with her, he let her. He figured he owed her the space. *Temporarily*, he assured himself.

She wrapped the sheet around herself, securing it in front and sat down in a chair near the bed. "Explain." Her voice was calm, but her hands shook as she twisted the sheet.

He sighed and sat up, raking his hand through his hair. "It's complicated."

"And I'm intelligent. Start talking."

He let that slide. "I followed you here. You know that much. When I walked into the hotel bar, you were already three sheets to the wind. You're a lightweight, Marley." He tried a smile. "Don't ever let anyone tell you different."

She didn't respond.

His smile faded. "There were all these guys on the prowl, circling you like vultures, and there you were, vulnerable and so drunk you could barely see straight. I don't think you even recognized me when I broke through to stand next to you at the bar." He shrugged. "So I just let the other guys think you were taken. And, after the auction, when it looked like a few guys still might not take no for an answer, I got desperate. You kept slipping away from me. So I slid a ring on your finger. Discreetly."

He grimaced. "And you know, even that didn't seem to faze some of them. Hell, right after the auction, I watched that guy with the toupee slip his *own* ring off before he approached you."

She glanced down at her hand, at the tiny diamond he'd enjoyed seeing there, more than he'd ever expected. Yanking the ring off, she flipped it onto the bed next to him. "I see. So do you usually carry an extra wedding ring with you?"

"Yes." He picked up the ring and looked at it. It was still warm from her skin. He felt the loss. "This was my mother's. I wore it on a chain around my neck until the other night."

Curiosity flashed momentarily in her eyes, but she just moved on to the next question. "You put me to bed?"

He swallowed heavily, remembering the strength of will it had taken to strip her out of her dress and underwear. He'd had no choice; her clothes had been soaking wet from a drink she'd spilled on herself when she'd stumbled.

If he were a saint, he might not have looked that extra moment, or let his hands linger that extra second on her slim back, the shapely legs. But he'd held himself to no more than that and slid her between the sheets, where she'd passed out.

"Yes, I put you to bed. No, nothing happened that

night. You were drunk and wearing most of your last drink."

"My clothes…" She glanced away, her cheeks burning. "So, the next morning. Why didn't you tell me the truth?"

"At first, it was just to make you squirm a little. You thought being married to me was hell on earth." He raised a shoulder, grimacing. "That stung a little. I had feelings for you. While you—" He shook his head, waving it off. "Anyway, I was going to let you off the hook, but then—"

He took a deep breath and met her gaze squarely. "But then I realized that you had given me the diversion I needed. Letting you continue to believe we'd married the night before would help me accomplish two things."

"Those being?" She coolly raised an eyebrow, but he could see the erratic throbbing of the pulse point at her throat.

He spoke quietly. "One—I needed to keep you out of Richmond for a while."

"Why?"

He made his voice as gentle as he could. "You're under suspicion for embezzlement."

"What?" She launched out of her chair.

"Settle down. This needs more explaining."

"I will *not* settle down. I didn't embezzle anything." Her voice shook. "I can't believe you would think that of me."

"I don't think it. I never did. Neither does your father." He paused, letting his words sink in. "We discovered all this right after you found out about Larry and quit your job. The timing of everything just made things look worse from an outsider's point of view. Your father and I knew you were already upset, so we wanted to try to clear this whole thing up without involving you."

She stared. "So I'm suspected of embezzling from my father's company and you thought you could handle it without involving me? Are you *nuts?*"

He shook his head. "You'd just quit your job. You'd split with your fiancé. You thought your father had betrayed you and I had humiliated you." He kept his voice level. "That's a lot to handle. And your dad and I felt responsible. We didn't want to add this embezzlement issue to the mess you faced."

"Oh, Lord." She covered her face. "And then I ran off to Vegas, so now everyone thinks I've been supporting a gambling habit. Right?"

He grimaced but didn't respond. She didn't need to hear all the gory details.

"So where do things stand now?"

"Not a lot better." He sighed, frustrated. "We think your ex-fiancé is the real culprit, but we don't have proof. I wanted to keep you busy here long enough for your father to find it."

Her smile was cold. "And were you supposed to sleep with me to keep me from suspecting anything? Tell me. Did my father reimburse you for *business* expenses?"

Furious, he stood up. "No, damn it, he did not and will not. This is my own doing. I'm here for you and nobody else. Except for me, maybe. Because I *wanted* to be with you."

She stood up, too, and made a grab for her clothes. Without looking at him, she slid her arms into the sleeves of her ruined blouse and tugged her skirt on. She wadded up the remainder and held it in front of her like a shield.

"So you didn't want to involve me in this investigation. And you think you had good reasons. Fine." She stared, hard. "But I'm involved now and I *will* clear my own name."

"Wait. There's more. It's about Larry."

Sighing with forced patience, she raised an eyebrow.

"You need to stay away from him. He could be dangerous. He has connections to organized crime and we think he's having you followed."

She pondered a moment, then gave a contemptuous snort. "Much you know."

"What does that mean?"

"None of your damned business. So now, if you'll excuse me, I need to go fix my screwed-up life."

Frustrated, he watched her turn and stalk toward the door. Just before she closed it behind her, she glanced back at him as though she couldn't help it. "So what was the second thing?"

"Second thing?"

She gestured impatiently. "You said there were two things you hoped to accomplish with this stupid marriage pretense."

He stepped closer, the hurt in her eyes compelling him forward. He needed to touch her. "I already told you. I wanted a chance to let you get to know me. Marley, I'm in love with you. Damn it, I *want* to be married to you." He reached out to her.

She glared and slammed the door in his face.

THE NEXT DAY FOUND Josh sitting in a chair, watching the elevator. Hard to believe it had been only a few days since he'd last waited for Marley in this chair. Today, she emerged looking cool and classy, but with a sassy tilt to her chin. She looked nervy, confident—no bowed head or hesitation. He was so proud of her he almost smiled. Until he saw other men glancing her way with more than casual interest. No. She was *his*, damn it.

When a bellhop followed her out pushing a cart loaded with her suitcase and various bags, Josh moved to overtake them.

"Get out of the way, Josh. I don't want to miss my flight."

"You won't. I'll hail a cab for us."

She glanced up sharply. "You don't need to follow me home. We're not married. Never have been, never will be."

"Marley—"

She shoved past him.

"Will you just *wait* a minute?" With an effort, he lowered his voice. "Be reasonable. This guy is still following you. He could be dangerous."

"No, he's not. And even if he were—" she spared him a cold glance "—he's *still* not your problem."

Josh gave her a shrewd look. "You know something."

"I know lots of somethings. Among them is the fact that this guy won't hurt me." She scowled with distaste. "Whether Larry sent him here or my father."

"I told you—"

"Enough!"

"Okay. I'm done. For now." He scrambled for an argument. "But we're both going to the airport. We both need a cab. It only makes sense to share. Come on." He tipped the bellhop and picked up her bags himself. She ignored him. Grimly determined, he followed in her wake and set her bags down next to his.

When a cab stopped and the bags were loaded, Josh turned to tip the bell captain. A door slammed behind him and the cab sped off. Déjà vu. Once again, he was staring at the taillights of a car driving Marley away from him.

"*Damn* it. The woman even took my luggage this time."

Fuming, he glanced at the bell captain, who shrugged, barely concealing a grin.

When he finally snagged a second cab and pulled up to curbside checking, he was further annoyed to find his bags sitting unattended on the pavement. It was just dumb luck that security hadn't impounded them yet.

The woman was obviously pissed.

Well so was *he* now.

He let his breath hiss through his teeth. Okay, so maybe she had more reason to be angry than he did. But he'd only been acting in her best interests. Surely she would realize that.

Meanwhile, he was going to miss his flight if he didn't hustle. He checked his baggage, got his boarding pass and found the right gate. They'd already begun loading. At this rate, he'd be lucky if his bags made it on the plane with him.

Boarding the plane, he scanned the passengers for an infuriating redhead then dropped down into the seat next to her.

She didn't even glance at him.

"That was a juvenile trick, Marley."

"Too bad it didn't work." She flipped the page of her magazine, her eyes intent on the next article. "You were supposed to miss the flight altogether. Yet here you are."

"You hate me that much now?"

She responded crisply. "Call me crazy. It seems I have a problem enduring a cross-country flight in company with a man who manipulated me, deceived me and slept with me. And who then let me humiliate myself further with a declaration of *undying love*." She flipped the next page.

The snide tone of her last statement was obviously self-directed. She must have been ripping herself to shreds inside. Josh winced, his temper cooling. He'd rather she only ripped into him. He deserved it.

"Marley. That declaration meant the world to me."

"Right." She spoke the one word in a deadpan voice then shook her head. "I can't believe I thought I was in love with a fraud like you. Obviously, I never learn."

"What do you mean you 'thought' you were in love with me? You've decided you're not?"

"Whether I am or not is completely moot. I don't know you, never did, and will avoid you in future. Now, do you mind? I'm trying to read."

"Yes, I do mind." He yanked the magazine out of her hands. "I'm in love with you. If you're honest with yourself, I think you'll admit that you're still in love with me, too. I know I screwed up. And I'm sorry. But I want you to understand that my intentions were good. Mostly. I wanted to protect you."

"Gee, I think it was that 'mostly' part that really pissed me off, though, Josh. The other stuff isn't too great, either. I really, really *hate* being manipulated."

Reading hurt in between glimmers of raw fury, he sighed. "I know, honey. I'm sorry. Let me make it up to you. Please."

"You want to make it up to me? Fine. *Do me no more favors.*" She shifted her gaze to front and center. "I have a rotten mess to clean up now, thanks to your meddling and my father's." She let out a frustrated snort. "Men. Cave dwellers, one and all."

He frowned at her. "Wait a minute. Your con of a boyfriend is the one who set you up, not your father and me. Hell, we were trying to fix everything for you."

"And that just brings up another reason why I'm angry right now." She turned to glare at him. "Who gave you the right to 'fix' *anything* for me, like I'm a little girl with a broken toy? I'm an *adult.* I'll solve my own damn problems."

He studied her a moment. "I take it you know how to solve this particular problem?"

She gave him an impatient look. "What do *you* think? I know the details of my files and my projects better than anyone else. I also know my scum of an ex better than you do."

He snorted.

She spoke over him. "At least in some respects. And—here's a shocker—I think I *even* know how he might have done it." She blinked guilefully, then tossed another glare at him. "So who all knows about this, anyway? Do I have any shreds of reputation left, or is it all gone, thanks to the three of you?"

He grimaced. "Your dad's been trying to keep a lid on it. There are probably rumors, though."

"That should do wonders for my career prospects. I imagine Larry's long gone by now?"

At that, he managed a grim smile. "Oh, no. Your dad hooked him with hints of bigger money and bigger clients. Donatelli's not going anywhere for a few weeks."

"Good. We should have all this cleared up in a matter of days then." She glanced at him pointedly. "No thanks to you. Now, if you don't mind, I'd like to do some reading."

"But, see, I do mind. What about us?"

"There is no 'us.'"

"Wrong. Less than eight hours ago, you told me you loved me. I told you the same thing. That spells 'us' to me."

She turned in her seat to face him and spoke in a furious whisper. "And *then* you told me you faked a wedding. How could you do that to me? I believed we were *married* when I had sex with you. God, I was such a fool. I was even willing to give our so-called *marriage* a chance. A marriage that didn't even exist. Do you know how *stupid* I feel right now?"

"You said the wedding wasn't even an issue. Or at least you implied it. You said you wanted me and *nothing else mattered.*"

She glared. "*Lies* matter, asshole. You *lied* to me. At least by omission. I trusted you enough to sleep with you and admit to having feelings for you. And you were *deceiving* me and keeping *secrets* from me the whole time. *That's* what pisses me off."

He was silent, staring at her. He shook his head wordlessly. "You're right. I'm sorry, Marley. I never meant to hurt you, and I didn't know what else to do at the time but… You're right. You deserved better than that."

"Yes, I *do*. And I'll *get* it, too, damn it."

His jealousy flared. "With someone like Larry, maybe?"

"Why not? What he's done is no worse than what you did." Her flippant words hit the mark with painful precision. "All he stole was money and a little pride. You stole what was left of my dignity and self-respect, and then you—" She broke off.

"I what?" He barely breathed the words, hoping. "What did I do, Marley?"

Her voice lowered. "You hurt me. You slept with me, even knowing—" She shook her head.

"Even knowing that you'd never slept with Larry." He'd guessed, and after the other night, he was pretty damned sure that was the case. She'd never even slept with her fiancé.

But she'd slept with Josh.

"That's none of your business." She snatched her magazine out of his hands and opened it. "Now leave me alone. Or do I need to ask the flight attendant to find me a different seat?"

"There aren't any open seats." And he was feeling contrary enough to tell her so.

She stared at him, obviously past endurance.

"Then I'll sit in the bathroom for the duration of the flight. Leave me alone. You owe me some peace."

He supposed he did. Sighing, he left her to her magazine. It was a silent flight, and he'd like to think that she occasionally let her gaze stray in his direction, but he wasn't sure. When the plane landed, she ignored him as though he were a stranger. She hurried off to claim her baggage. He found, to no great surprise, that his had taken a detour, probably by way of Dallas. He'd have his bags in a day or two, he was told.

Muttering about the consistency of bad days, he picked up his carry-on and headed off to the garage.

Marley saw him moments later as she was maneuvering her own car out of the parking garage. He was kicking what looked to be one of four flat tires on his car. A prank, probably. She smiled grimly. She hadn't done it, but he certainly had it coming.

The temptation was overwhelming, but she refused the opportunity to leave him to his misery. She stopped her car next to him and popped her trunk. Moments later, it slammed shut and he slid into her passenger seat.

"Thanks." He sounded humble.

Good. Let's see who feels helpless and stupid now.

Without glancing at him further, she exited the garage and found her way to the interstate. It was six o'clock, and already getting dark, given the time of year. She exited to downtown and glanced at him briefly. "I'm stopping by the office to pick up the stuff Pattie boxed up for me. With your permission, I'd also like to go through some files while I'm there. I might be able to give you the evidence you need against Larry."

"All right." He spoke quietly, thoughtfully.

She nodded and continued driving. In the continued silence, she felt her fury—the emotion that had gotten her this far and this fast—ebbing dangerously. She couldn't bear to look at him for too long now. It hurt, more and more, thinking about how he'd humiliated her, whatever his reasons. And the worst part was she'd wanted so badly to believe in the fantasy.

For a while, she'd felt she had happily-ever-after in her grasp. Love, passion, laughter, adventure. For a few, wonderful moments in time, she'd thought she had it all, despite the vague beginnings. She'd thought she'd lucked into something fantastical. And she had. It had all been fantastical, as in surreal, as in not real, as in *all in her head.*

She wondered what other lies he'd let her believe. *I'm in love with you. Damn it, I want to be married to you.*

Minutes later, she parked the car and reached beneath her seat for the briefcase she kept there. They walked up the front steps and paused at the door while Josh unlocked it for her. They rode the elevator, a silent, long ride, up to what had been her office until only a few days ago.

Light shone from beneath the door.

She paused with her hand on the knob. Had they already moved someone else in? She glanced questioningly at Josh, but he shook his head, his eyes grim.

She set her jaw and shoved the door open. A man glanced up, startled. He was sitting at the desk that used to be hers, and looking very much at home there. The sight made her pause, but only briefly. She walked in.

"Marley." The man looked frozen in place, but for pale blue eyes that shifted nervously from Marley to Josh. Then back to Marley before widening and dropping.

"Larry." Marley sighed. She'd known. But it still sucked to be right sometimes. "What are you doing here?"

"Huh? Oh." He glanced at the computer screen. "I mean, what are *you* doing here? You said you'd resigned." He glanced down, his fingers flying briefly over the keyboard.

Eyes sharpening, she strode quickly around the desk. "You were listening. How unusual. So tell me then, since I have your attention. What are you trying to download from my computer?"

He tapped a few more keys in rapid succession and looked up, his expression bland. "I'm just following through on a few things. Someone had to take up the slack when you took off. That was a pretty juvenile trick, Marley. Leaving like that."

"Right." Seeing what was now a blank screen, she shielded her emotions and dug into her briefcase. "Looking for this?"

She held up a floppy disk with a clearly printed label. *Blaylock.* Her pet project, the details of which she hadn't yet passed on to her father—but which she'd occasionally allowed Larry to handle for her. He was good at handling vendors, for example, coming up with quotes and authorizing checks in her name for services rendered.

She saw his jaw tighten, his gaze drawn irresistibly to the disk. Bingo. She'd been right. "You bastard. You *have* been falsifying invoices, haven't you."

He narrowed his eyes. "You can't prove anything."

"No?" Her voice was cool. *"Watch me."*

She turned back to Josh, who'd been watching her with quiet intensity. "How much has he taken?"

"About $165,000 over the past six months. And you're probably right about the invoices." He glanced briefly at Larry. "KTL Consulting doesn't exist. From what we can gather, Larry here has been authorizing payment in your name."

"No, wait." Larry stood up, shifting nervously, his eyes wide and drifting between Marley and Josh. Finally he settled, pleadingly, on Marley. "I can explain."

"Don't bother." She gave him a pitying look. "I can't believe it. You actually stole from my father's company and then you were going to let me take the blame for it."

"No! Well...maybe for a while, but you would have been cleared. And even if you weren't, you know the *almighty Charles Brentwood*—" he sneered "—wouldn't send his daughter to jail."

"Shut up, Larry."

"Even if she is a tramp who flies off to Vegas for a sleazy affair with her fiancé's co-worker." He flashed her an angry but triumphant look. "From frigid bitch to slut. Overnight."

"You'll pay for that." Josh lunged for him, but Marley grabbed his arm.

"Josh. Stop it. For once—God, just for *once*—let me handle my own damned life."

Josh looked pissed off and torn, but he held his ground.

She turned back to Larry. "Now you. How did you get your information about Las Vegas? Or do I even need to ask? You sent that creep to follow me, didn't you."

He gave her a resentful glance. "No, my *father* did."

"*Your* father?"

He smirked. "Damn. You thought it was Brentwood."

"It had to be you or him. Or so I thought."

"Nope. My old man was checking up on me and my *bride-to-be*." He gave her a poisonous look. "And he just loved like hell filling me in on the details. Sent his most inept little goon to follow you, and boy, did he come back with hot information."

Marley pondered for just a moment. "So the verdict is that I'm a slut? That I ran off to Las Vegas with my father's vice president to have kinky sex and gamble away the family fortune?"

"You got it." Larry gave her a hateful smile.

How about that? *Rational ice princess Marley enjoys her first vice-laden scandal, as reported by the criminal underworld to her weasel of an ex-fiancé.* She smiled, just a little.

Seeing it, Josh gave her a disgruntled look. "You like?"

She raised her nose in the air. "I do like."

"What the hell?" Larry glanced between them. "This is good? That people think you're a *slut* as well as a thief?"

Josh moved forward threateningly. "You'd better find some respect, Donatelli, and fast."

"*Josh*—" Marley growled under her breath.

But Larry was already repenting. "I'm sorry. I'm sorry." He tossed his hands up. "Maybe it just stung a little. To hear about you and Vegas from my old man. You know he couldn't give a rat's ass what happens to me. Just wants to rub my nose in it and everything else I screw up."

"He's a *criminal*, Larry. What do you care?"

"I *don't*, damn it. But I wanted to show him up and—"

Marley groaned. "I knew it. You're trying to prove something to him."

"No, get *back* at him. There's a difference."

She gave him a narrow look. "Revenge on daddy. That's your whole reason for embezzling. My God, when I found out about the connection between you two and asked you about it, you said you were estranged from him. That you wanted to be as far away from organized crime as you could get. But you were lying."

"No—"

"Yes. You wanted back in so bad you were will-

ing to steal from my father to do it. Just so you could
make Daddy Donatelli sorry and realize what a
good little criminal you could be. That's pathetic,
Larry."

And her words suddenly made her feel hollow as
hell. Who'd have thought she and Larry would end
up so much alike? He embezzled to get back at
Daddy. And Marley... Well, that whole stupid mess
in Las Vegas was a sorry excuse for a rebellion against
her own father. A rebellion she should have con-
ducted on a smaller scale and with less disastrous ef-
fects when she was *thirteen*—not twenty-eight.

But at least she was paying the price for her own
behavior.

So should Larry.

Ignoring Josh for the moment, Marley planted her
hands on the desk and gave Larry her full attention.
"Your father is your problem. All I care about is the
embezzlement and my reputation. You are not going
to make *me* pay for *your* crimes."

"Oh, come on, Marley." He lowered his voice per-
suasively, leaning forward so only she could hear. "I
have a plan. Much bigger than all this. Your dad
won't miss the money. You know he won't. And I can
put it to good use. Hell, my dad's a criminal. Anything I did here's small potatoes compared to what
he does. But he'll see. I'll make him pay. You know
he has it coming."

"Maybe he does. Again, not my problem."

"But Marley—"

"Shut up and pay attention. Here's what you're
going to do. First you'll present a money order to my
father in the amount of $165,000, plus ten percent in-
terest. I think that's conservative, frankly, considering what my father could have gotten for it by
investing. But it's a good off-the-cuff number. If the
money's not here by noon tomorrow, then I believe

my father's vice president here will report your theft to the District Attorney's office." She raised an eyebrow at Josh.

He nodded silently. "We'll review your expense account and company credit-card charges, and anything in the least questionable will be added to that number Miss Brentwood quoted you. I should have that total for you by 10:00 a.m. That should give you plenty of time to get to the bank and back here with a money order." He raised an eyebrow. "I'll update the attorneys, too, so we'll be all set to file charges against you if necessary."

She flashed a cool smile at Larry. "I guess that's it. Hand over the keys, surrender your company cards and get out."

"Why should I?" Larry relaxed back in his chair. He looked at Marley. "You no longer work for this company." His glance shifted to Josh. "And I don't work for you."

Josh moved forward, but Marley held him off again. "I'm not done." She gritted the words out to Josh before turning back to Larry. "True enough. I don't have any authority over you in the company. Try this on for size, though. If you make any kind of fuss, I'll be suing you personally for framing me. I think they call it defamation of character?"

He glared. "You can't do that. My father—"

"*Will do nothing.* Remember?" She raised an eyebrow.

He turned away with a curse.

They both knew his threats were empty. Marley could almost pity the guy. He should have gone adventuring years ago.

And ended up in her shoes instead?

Grimacing, she turned and left the office, leaving Josh to deal with the details while she waited downstairs.

Several minutes later, Josh escorted Larry from the building. Larry, whose eye seemed swollen all of a sudden, trudged off to his car, looking defeated.

Josh joined Marley and they got into her sedan. After they watched Larry's car blaze off, Josh turned to her. New respect shone from his eyes. "That was one hell of a performance."

She glanced at him but didn't return his smile. "Just laid the facts out for him. I'm pretty confident you can find the documents backing everything up on that disk I gave you. And by calling our contractors." She shook her head. "I just feel like an idiot for trusting him, almost marrying him even."

"He put on a good act—even fooled your father."

"Maybe. I would've loved to call the police on him, but—"

He sighed. "Not good for the company. Not now."

"I know." She gave him a wry look. "Any plans for preventing him from stealing from anyone else?"

"You know your father. He has influence in the business community. He'll let word get around that Larry has closer ties to his dad than he does. That should take care of it."

"I guess that will have to do. That and the black eye you gave him." She gave him a sidelong glance, saw satisfaction wash over his face. Men, animals. Pretty much one and the same beast.

Not commenting further, she started the car and followed his directions to his house. Once there, she pulled into the driveway and parked, engine still running. Unless she was mistaken, that was her father's car parked in the street, too.

"Come in with me." He spoke quietly.

She shook her head.

"Please. At least meet Lance."

Amusement nudged at her briefly then disappeared. "It's not a good idea."

"You're afraid of a bird?"

"Did my father really take care of him?" She studied him with reluctant curiosity.

Josh glanced at her father's car, smiling a little. "Yeah, he did." His smile faded, his eyes growing serious again. "Marley, I didn't lie to you about anything. Honest. I just let you believe what you decided on your own. Everything else—my feelings, my bird, my history, everything—was true. *Is* true."

She stared at him.

"Come and meet Lance. You can talk soaps with him."

She sighed and gave in. "I'll come in for a moment." Seeing the satisfaction glinting in his eyes, she narrowed her own and clarified. "Because it's convenient. My father's here and I need to talk to him about Larry and the Blaylock project."

Not commenting, he held out a hand to her and helped her out of the car.

Eyeing the small carry-on he'd grabbed out of her trunk, she frowned. "That's it? What about the rest of your—" A glance at his narrowed eyes was all she needed. She bit her lip.

"My bags? They're most likely spending the night in Texas, according to the airline. If they'd been checked when your cab arrived, they might have made it to RIC, just like yours did."

She nodded, a little rush of satisfaction soothing her shattered ego. "It's no more than you deserve."

"Still riding that power kick, huh? Funny how busting an embezzler will do that for you, I guess." His lips quirked.

Glaring briefly, she stalked into the house and froze in quiet surprise. Josh slowed to a halt just behind her.

From the living-room couch, a familiar voice echoed with enthralled disgust. "I can't believe Sirena let him get away with that. Doesn't she know he's just using her? Shit. I thought the woman had more balls than that."

Gesturing angrily at the TV, Charles Brentwood dug a hand in the open bag of M&M's on his lap. A large, blue bird with a handsome yellow chest and hooked beak perched on Charles's shoulder. It squawked as if in agreement with its companion's words, then ducked its black beak into Charles's shirt pocket.

Shocked, Marley just shook her head, amazed to see her no-nonsense father sprawled on the couch with chocolate, an exotic bird and a soap opera. "Dad?"

He leaped off the couch, with Lance shrieking and spreading his wings. As Charles harrumphed through his discomfort and set the bag of candy on a lamp table, Josh coaxed the bird onto his arm and out of harm's way. He turned off the TV.

The bird squawked and raised its magnificent beak, wings poised just so. It was a maestro commanding attention before the performance. "*Sirena. My one and only love.*" Lance shrieked. "*Just give me tonight.*"

After a moment of appreciative silence, Charles managed to shift his fascinated gaze from the bird. He cleared his throat and concentrated on his daughter. "Marley, you're back."

A little bemused still, Marley forced herself to focus. "Yes. I'm back." She glanced around before tossing her purse on the couch where her father had been sitting. Then she faced him. "I cleaned up your mess."

"My mess?" He frowned at her.

"Larry." She felt her ire rising again but kept her voice even. "And, by the way, since I no longer work there, I guess you could say I just broke into your office—"

"I let her in." Josh interrupted.

"—blackmailed your employee—"

"With the truth."

"—and told him you would be expecting reimbursement by noon tomorrow. If he failed, you'd file charges with the D.A.'s office. I didn't fire him, though. That's your job." Marley smiled coolly at her father.

"*I* fired him, then confiscated his keys and company cards." Josh spoke quietly from behind her. "I assumed you would back me up."

"Good." Charles exhaled heavily. "I'm glad that's settled. Marley, we need to talk."

"About what?"

Josh frowned briefly. "My guess is he wants you to come back to Brentwood Electronics."

"I'm not coming back to that job."

"You shouldn't." Charles's voice rang with certainty.

"What?" Josh and Marley spoke in unison.

Charles shoved his hands in his pockets. "I mean it. I've been giving this some thought. You shouldn't take your old job back. Do what you want to do. Don't work for your old man, because I keep underestimating you." He shrugged as she continued to stare at him in shock. "The whole department has gone to hell since you left. Another company—hell, I could name you two of them, off the top of my head—would snatch you up in a heartbeat." He grimaced. "Damn phone's been ringing off the hook. Did you really give my name as a reference?"

She raised an eyebrow. "You were my boss. Why wouldn't I?"

"You quit and I didn't want you to."

She shrugged. "You still wouldn't give me a bad reference. Not unless I deserved it."

He nodded. "Thanks for that."

"This humble act of yours is making me nauseous, Charles."

Marley's father smiled crookedly at Josh. "How the hell do you think it makes *me* feel?"

Josh laughed.

Sobering, Charles gave him a probing look. "You do good work, too, Walker. You got my daughter back here in one piece. The embezzler's been found out. I guess we can sign the papers tomorrow. You've got yourself a company, son."

Marley whirled to stare accusingly at Josh, then glared at her father. "Oh, this is rich. I take care of everything for both of you and he gets the credit? So much for the humility act—and not underestimating your daughter." She snatched up her purse and turned to go. "Bumbling males. You deserve each other's company."

"*Oh, to hell with men and everything they stand for.*" Lance's chest swelled with pride as he carefully whistled his way through syllables. "*Duplicitous, manipulative wretches.*"

Marley glanced at the feathered sage with new respect. "You've got that right, bird. Good luck with them."

12

When the door closed behind her, Josh turned back to his boss with a glare. "Nice work, Charles."

"*Ki-iss me, my darling—*" squawk "—*I want to make love to yo-ou.*" Lance tucked his beak under a wing.

"Damn lech." Muttering it with a reluctant grin, Charles harrumphed himself into a brow-wrinkling frown and focused on Josh. "Would it do any good to remind you that I am still the man who signs the checks and that I haven't yet signed the papers giving you my company?"

Josh raised an eyebrow at the man he'd called both boss and friend. "According to our contract, you're hardly 'giving' me the company. And you never paid me to be your yes-man." The response was halfhearted, though. His thoughts still centered on the woman who seemed intent on stalking out of his life.

"*Damn lech.*"

Josh glanced up in surprise. Feathers rustled innocently. "You've been corrupting my bird, too?"

Charles cast a harassed look at Lance. "I've got news for you, son. That bird's already corrupt."

Josh just shook his head.

Charles coughed and snorted, his mind obviously drifting to serious matters. "So. What's going on with you and my daughter?"

Josh dropped all semblance of good humor, his

eyes on his bird now as it bent its feathered head for a good scratching. Josh obliged, his tension easing slightly. He'd missed the little pervert.

"Well?" Charles spoke impatiently.

Josh looked at him. "I'm in love with her. And thanks to you, she hates me."

"Thanks to me?"

"In part. Most women refuse to date men their fathers try to buy for them. They also have a problem with manipulation and deception, and Marley's had more than her share of that recently." He cocked his head with new realization. "Plus, I think I reminded her of you in some ways."

Charles glanced away. "And that's probably your worst offense." He dropped back onto the couch. "Damn." Charles raised his hands and lowered them, his frustration obvious. "I've never known how to deal with her. Once her mother died, I was left with this little girl and just didn't know what to do with her."

"Until she went into the business."

Charles flashed him a glance of perfect accord. "Sure. Everything clicked into place then. I understood her. At least I thought I did. I'm proud of her. She's smart as hell. The most dedicated marketing director the company's ever—"

"She's your *daughter*, Charles."

"I *know*. I made some mistakes, but she knows I love her and I'm proud of her." He stood abruptly, a rueful grin on his face. "Hell, I sound like a weepy woman. I've been watching too many of those shows with that bird of yours." He shook his head. "Smart as a whip, isn't he?"

"Twisted but smart."

Charles snorted with brief amusement before sobering. "I meant what I said, though. We can sign papers in the morning."

Will it make you happy? Marley's question echoed

in his mind. Josh didn't know. He'd had his eyes so firmly on the goal—Brentwood Electronics—that he'd never stopped to wonder where he'd go from there. It was the pinnacle of his career plan. *But what then?* Good question.

Josh turned from him and set the bird on a perch inside its cage. He let his thoughts turn over in his head. He could think of only one way to show Marley that he wanted her and loved her. One way to make it up to her. He turned back to Charles.

"I'm not buying your company." He spoke the words slowly, but as soon as he said them, he knew it was the right thing to do—both for Marley and for himself. She was right.

Charles frowned at him. "Why the hell not? What's wrong with my company?"

Josh smiled slightly. "Not a thing, now that your daughter's cleaned house for you."

"A few months ago, you were ready to bust my door down to get inside the executive office. Now that I'm offering it to you, you're turning me down. What's your problem, Walker?"

"My problem is that I'm in love with your daughter. I want her more than I want that company of yours."

"LORD, WHAT AN ADVENTURE." Samantha was still laughing, her eyes bemused. "So you're married but not married, you dodge a Mafia-stalker type, and then you come home and blackmail your embezzling ex-fiancé? Who needs *Worlds of Passion* when we can all just live in the world of Marley?"

"Funny, Sammi." Marley turned back to the suitcase she was unpacking. Lifting out her new sequined dress, she paused, remembering that magical night she and Josh had spent fulfilling her dreams of adventure. Then she remembered seeing the dress in a shiny heap on his hotel-room floor as she kicked out of it. The look in Josh's eyes then still made her knees weak. He'd looked hungry enough to pounce.

Except *she'd* done the pouncing. Her face flamed. "What?"

Marley glanced away. "I'm in love with Josh."

Silence. Samantha stared at her.

"And I never want to see him again."

After another silent moment, Samantha just shook her head and burrowed deeper into the pillows on Marley's bed. "I'm just going to sell my TV and move in with you."

"I'm serious, Sammi." Marley glanced at her, knowing her misery was written all over her face.

"Oh, boy." Samantha sat up, her smile gone. "How in love?"

Marley frowned. "What do you mean? I'm in love. Period."

"In love with the way he made you feel, in love with great sex, in love until something better comes along or in love and nothing's ever going to be the same again?"

Marley sighed. "That last one."

"Uh-oh."

Marley nodded.

"Then why won't you see him again?"

Marley frowned at her cousin. "Haven't you been listening to me? I told you about his deception, the way he manipulated me. The way he let me go on believing horrible things about myself. How can I ever trust him again? How can I possibly believe him when he says he loves me? For all I know, he's another Larry. We've already seen how gullible I can be."

"But Josh did all these things because he wanted to protect you, right? From other guys and from what was happening in Brentwood Electronics."

She shrugged. "Sure, he says he did it all to protect me. Except for the part where I threw up and it offended his pride."

"What?" Samantha grinned again, then forced a more sober expression. "We'll get to that part later. The other stuff is true, though, right? He was trying to buy time and keep you safe and sane?"

"More or less." The admission came grudgingly.

"Call me a romantic idiot, but I don't think he's anything like Larry. I think you ought to give him another chance."

Marley raised an eyebrow but didn't respond.

"So now that we have that settled, I want to hear how you vomited on his pride." Sammi's grin was completely unrepentant.

Marley rolled her eyes but grinned and started talking.

Twenty minutes later, the doorbell rang and Marley exchanged a glance with her cousin. *Who now?* Marley's heart started racing. *Josh?*

Not sure whether she'd be turning him away or inviting him in to heap more abuse on his head, Marley glanced out the window to see who it was. False alarm. She went to open the door.

"Hi, Dad." Marley stepped back and let him in. He looked around curiously and Marley just waited, feeling odd. Her father had visited her apartment only a few times since she'd moved in several years ago. She usually saw him only at the office.

"Hi, Uncle Charles." Samantha spoke in a shameless singsong. Marley suppressed a smile. Her cousin generally used that particular tone to dance all over his nerves.

Charles smiled down at his niece and accepted her kiss on his cheek. "Hello, young lady. So what trouble are you and my daughter stirring up now?"

"Trouble? What trouble?" Sammi smiled angelically.

He shook his head sadly but the smile remained.

"Was there something on your mind, Dad?" Marley spoke quietly. Her thoughts drifted back to her father's offer to sell his company to Josh.

Charles turned back to his daughter. "Yes. There is, actually." He studied her face for a moment, a strange warmth in his eyes. Neither noticed when Samantha wished them a casual farewell and left.

Uncomfortable under this unusual scrutiny, Marley found it hard to hold his gaze. "I'm listening."

"You're a beautiful woman." His eyes were musing, his words softly gruff.

Marley's eyes widened.

"Just like your mother." Shifting a little, he still held her gaze. She could tell it was hard for him. His cheeks were flushed, his words uncomfortable but obviously sincere. "I guess that's why it's been so hard to deal with you over the years."

She nodded speechlessly.

He harrumphed and rocked on his heels. "I'm here because I changed my mind. I want you to come back and work for me."

"I already quit, Dad." She spoke quietly, but there was no edge to her voice. He'd stunned her. Three sentences together that had nothing to do with business. And he'd mentioned her mother, something he rarely did.

"I want you back. I'm willing to match your other offers, even give you a promotion."

She studied him. "Why?"

He frowned. "Because you're a damn good businesswoman. You know the company inside and out and you work harder than anyone else on staff. And you're my daughter. I want you back."

She continued to study him. "I need something different."

"Like what? A raise? More responsibility?"

It came together at once. She knew what she wanted. "I want to be the boss."

His mouth quirked and he appraised her all over again. "Boss, huh? After resigning from the company? There's nerve."

"Well, why would you rehire me anyway?" She grew angry all over again. "You're selling the company to Josh. Interesting that you never once even *mentioned* that possibility to me. Why are you selling it, anyway? And why to him, of all people?"

Her father folded his arms across his chest. "It's time. The challenge isn't really there for me anymore, and I've started letting things go. Josh was right. This embezzlement was at least partly my fault. I should have kept a better eye on management, but I guess I just left things in Donatelli's hands because it was easier. He wanted the responsibility and I gave him the opportunity to abuse it. I'm sorry you got hurt."

Marley nodded quietly. "So you're retiring?"

"It's time."

"If that's what you want."

"It is." He smiled. "So it's okay with you if I sell the company to Josh?"

"No."

His smile widened and his eyes grew speculative. "I guess you'll be happy to know he's already turned me down, then."

"He did?"

"Flat-out."

"But why?" She gave him an affronted look. "What's wrong with the company?"

Charles guffawed, but just shook his head when she raised a questioning eyebrow.

"Well, what is it, then? I know he wanted to buy it before." Surely he didn't do that just because of her— "He found another company. Or he's trying to drive your price down."

Charles was already shaking his head. "He did it because of you. He won't buy my company. I did everything but stand on my fool head trying to hand it over to him after you left, but he wouldn't budge."

"He just…gave it up? Just like that?" Her stomach dropped. "For me?"

"Just like that. For you."

She glanced away, paced across the room, then back again. "Tell me exactly what he said."

"I think you should ask him yourself." Charles studied his daughter, and she couldn't find one comfortable place to rest her gaze or her mind. She couldn't believe it.

Annoyed by her indecision, she snatched up her purse. "Okay, I will."

"Good. Oh, and Marley…"

She glanced back, distracted.

He smiled. "You can start on Monday."

Her eyes widened.

His narrowed. "You want to be the boss? Fine. I'll show you how to do it. Now that you scared away my buyer, you're my only shot at a decent retirement." He paused. "Josh gave me the details of what happened with Larry. You handled yourself well."

While she just gaped at him, he lowered his eyebrows in a mock frown. "We can iron out a contract on Monday. Just go take care of your personal life so you can concentrate on business."

"So, Lance, what kind of odds do you give me? Two to one says Marley avoids me until I go after her myself." Grimacing at the watchful macaw, Josh shoved his hands in his pockets. He couldn't give her too much time to think or she'd rebuild her defenses against him and he'd never get through to her again.

Strategy. He had to think strategy.

As he contemplated the merit of a simple show-down at her apartment, he heard the doorbell ring.

"Sirena, my love." The squawking voice lowered in pitch. *"Shut up, ya damn lech."*

Josh groaned and laughed. Apparently, this was a phrase that would stick. Shaking his head, he went to answer the door.

"Marley." She'd trumped him.

Before he could comment on her presence, she breezed past him without closing the door. "I have questions for you."

"Oh. Well, come on in and make yourself at home, then." He shut the door.

Not commenting on his ironic tone, she halted on the other side of the room and whirled to face him. "My father said you're not buying his company."

Business. Damn. "That's true. I don't want to buy his company." As he studied her a moment, his mood improved dramatically. Not business at all, he decided, fascinated by the upset he could see in her rapid breathing and fidgeting fingers. Sighting opportunity, he moved.

"Why? Why did you do this?" She stared at him, not commenting on or reacting to his gradual approach. "All you've wanted from the beginning was my father's company. You told me so yourself."

As subtly as he could allow, he closed in on her. He had the woman back in his home, right where he wanted her. Damned if he'd be letting her go again. "What did your father tell you?"

She shifted restlessly. "He said you did it for me."

"What else did he tell you?"

Her eyes were huge as he stopped inches away from her. "He said you wanted me more than the company."

"Also true." He lowered his voice. "But that's not all. I'm in love with you. I have been for months. To

hell with the job, the company, the city and everything else that's standing between us. All I want in
this whole screwed-up world is you."

Her eyes flickered and she ducked under his arm,
retreating to the other side of the room. "None of this
makes any sense."

He pivoted to track her with his eyes. "It's not
supposed to make sense. It's called love. Emotion.
Risk. Adventure. It's not supposed to be logical. It
just is what it is."

Her lips curved slightly, though she continued to
fidget. "The philosopher again."

"Take it or leave it."

"Do I have a choice?"

"I suppose you could think so." No. No choices.
She'd take him if he had to tie her to his bed and keep
her there until she gave in. He smiled, just thinking
about persuasion tactics.

She raised her chin. "Spell it out, Josh."

"All right." He tugged the chain over his head
and unclasped it to remove his mother's ring. He'd
been wearing it since she left his hotel room, on the
same chain he'd worn for years now. But his path
had deviated dramatically from the one he'd chosen
as a youth. Instead of leading him away from his father's failures, it led him directly to his own future.
Her. "Will you marry me?"

She stared a moment, her throat working before
she spoke in a husky voice. "You call that romance?"

Noting the change in her manner, he grinned.
Things were definitely looking up. "You want romance? Say yes and I'll show you romance."

Her eyes narrowed, but he saw her lips quivering
slightly. "Are you by any chance attempting to ma-
nipulate me into giving you the answer you want?
I'm not real fond of manipulation."

"No kidding."

He watched her glance around the room before focusing on a deck of cards lying on a small table by the window. He'd bought it as a souvenir from the casino they'd patronized.

She smiled slowly.

Uh-oh.

"You know, everyone's been telling me I rely too much on control and planning. That I'm predictable. Unfailingly *rational*. Well, you know what? I'm tired of being trapped inside this reputation. It's boring and, frankly, it's just not working for me anymore." She smiled pleasantly, but her eyes were nervy.

Oh, hell.

"So I have a proposition for you." Her voice was cool.

He moved closer. "What is it?"

"First, is your proposal sincere? Or were you thinking in terms of another counterfeit relationship?" She eyed him with provoking condescension.

"Oh, it's real all right. Give me five minutes and I'll show you just how real my intentions are." He reached for her, but she ducked under his arm and glided over to the table.

She picked up the cards and smiled briefly at him. "I'm proposing a card game. With a different kind of wager. I wasn't very good at blackjack, so I think we'll keep this simple."

His heart thudded sickly.

"It goes like this. If you hold the high card, we get married." She paused. "If the bank holds the high card, we don't."

"That's crazy, Marley."

"Irrational maybe?" She raised an eyebrow.

His heart sank. "Completely."

She smiled. "Good. Ready?"

"You're the bank?"

"I still like control. Risk is okay, but I like control. *I'm* the bank and *I'll* deal the cards."

Well, at least his odds were better now. Fifty-fifty. Whatever the outcome, though, he had no intention of letting her get away so easily. She was his. And he was hers.

Still, she deserved to be in the driver's seat this time, if possible. They'd try things her way first. He nodded his agreement and she shuffled the cards with quick, deft movements.

Her actions brought to mind a scene he'd witnessed that first night in Vegas. He'd watched Marley, already a few drinks past go, talking to a seasoned gambler in the bar. The man had been showing Marley something with cards. Blackjack maybe. Josh shook his head slowly, remembering the night.

Aside from the jealousy he'd felt at seeing Marley enjoy herself with another man, he'd loved watching her. She'd smiled and laughed, her eyes sparkling with intrigue. It had been his first glimpse of the relaxed Marley he'd seen more of each day.

A snap of the cards recalled his attention, and he realized she'd dealt one to each of them.

Marley turned her card over first. A jack of diamonds. She looked up at him, her expression veiled.

His jaw tightened. The odds were obviously against him now. "Marley, this is nuts. You win or lose money over cards. Not a relationship. Not *love*."

"You agreed to this. Let's see the card, Josh."

Cursing under his breath, Josh flipped the card over. A queen of hearts. Their gazes met and locked. Slowly, her lips curved into a smile.

Married.

He reached for her and, with a wicked grin, she met him halfway. It was the same expression she'd worn at the casino, and it entranced him all over again despite his near-violent relief. He silenced her laughter with a hard, punishing kiss. When he came up for air, they were both breathless and she was leaning most of her weight against him.

"Don't you ever scare me like that again."

"Well, *I* think you deserved it."

"Maybe."

"No maybe about it." She raised an eyebrow at him. "That sham marriage was a rotten trick to play on a woman, no matter what your reasons for doing it."

He nodded, his mouth twisting a little. "After watching you handle Larry, I'll have to admit I screwed up big-time."

She leaned her forehead against his chin. "And, since we're all eating humble pie, I'll concede that your intentions were good." She leaned back and glanced up at him, her eyes puzzled. "Especially now that you've decided not to buy Dad's company. That's what made me think twice about it."

"I see."

She smiled. "So. Since you're not buying the company…" Her smile turned teasing. "You can start treating me with more respect. Come Monday, I'll be taking over as boss."

He grinned in surprise. "No way." He threw his head back and laughed. "Was this your idea or your father's?"

"Mine." She raised an eyebrow. "But I'll have some specific demands to go in that contract before I sign it. I won't be under his thumb anymore. I need his guidance until I learn the ropes, but I won't be a puppet forever."

"Good for you." He gave her another hard kiss.

When they parted, she stared up into his eyes. "Will it be a problem? You working for me instead of my father?" She inhaled deeply and met his eyes. "Josh, I know what owning this company would mean to you, and…" She paused and spoke quietly. "Frankly, it's enough that you made the gesture for my sake, but I won't hold you to it. If you want the company, you should go ahead and buy it if my father's still willing. I can make my own way. It was my original plan anyway, so—"

"I'm not buying your father's company, Marley."

"You're sure?" When he nodded, she smiled. "So you won't mind working for me?" Her grin widened. "Your wife?"

He chuckled. "I won't mind at all. But you might be finding a replacement for me at some point. You've given me ideas."

"What do you mean?"

"Well, I've been thinking about it, and I like your idea. I think I will look into freelancing as a consultant." He grinned. "An expensive one."

She laughed and rolled her eyes. "Just don't let it go to your head."

"I won't." His smile faded, to be replaced by a curious look. "I have to know. What if I had drawn the low card?"

She raised her chin and her eyes narrowed to sleepy, satisfied slits. "It wouldn't have happened. I stacked the deck. Some risks are worth taking. But no way would I risk forfeiting a lifetime adventure with you."

If you enjoyed what you just read,
then we've got an offer you can't resist!

Take 2 bestselling love stories FREE!

Plus get a FREE surprise gift!